WHERE LOVE MEETS WAR

Book 1: OF MIND OR MATTER

by Sreejit Poole

Cover art by painter Sree Subha Madhusudanan

[handwritten signature]

Check out
"The Seeker's Dungeon"
sreejit's Blog

Special thanks to the Artist Sree Subha Madhusudanan for the cover painting.

Chapter 1

Often, it seems the most beautiful and potent experiences come after first rising up and freeing ourselves from the grips of the most terrible despair. So begins my own endurance of this path of resurrection. Not wanting to rehash my early years in all their glory, I will just tell you that I had reached a point in my life where the thought of the utter futility and worthlessness of my existence was completely consuming my every action. Unwilling to continue like this, I committed myself to drastic measures.

My uncertainty about the hereafter kept me from ever seriously considering suicide. I instead satisfied my depression with mere fatalistic fantasies, lacking the will to carry them out. I knew, however, that I had to make certain changes in my life to bring about a death to the person I had become, in order to create a more worthy individual in its place. You see, my life was completely lacking - lacking commitment, lacking goals, lacking purpose, lacking the passion to do anything – and I was tired of walking that same path of nothingness for no reason other than not knowing what else to do with myself. Even if I were motivated purely towards seeking pleasure, it would have been better than the complete and total inertia that overcame my life. I wanted passion. I couldn't tell you what I wanted passion for, as that was exactly my problem, but I wanted a strong passion for something – for knowledge, or ice cream sundaes or the smiles of a beautiful face. Something... Anything... With this in mind, I decided to do something different. I decided to begin again.

On this Monday morning, I packed one suitcase of clothes, a backpack with some odds and ends, and a flask of coffee and left my downtown San Diego, California apartment for the last time. I loaded up my Oldsmobile and headed north on Interstate 5. I wasn't thinking about anything except saving myself through destroying myself. I had to sever my identity with a life I hated, in order to find out if I had anything inherent within me that was worth living for.

While driving, I made a solemn vow never to return to the place from where I left. I was hurtling myself at seventy miles per hour towards an uncertain future. Although nothing awaited me, I knew it couldn't be any worse than what I was giving up. Even if I were to die of starvation, I would at least know I was dying with the intention of doing something great, which was better than living with no intention at all. I felt both liberated and scared, but my fear only served to motivate me.

I drove in silence for about three hours. I was committed to staying awake until I'd reached my unknown destination, but the coffee soon wore off. I turned the radio to full volume, having left my extensive CD collection behind. I loved jazz, but found some boring top 40 station that served the purpose. As the hours passed, my mind raced towards all that I was leaving. I had no friends. Well, I should say rather that I had no one for whom I would give my life, or for that matter even invite over for dinner. I was fortunate in some respects. I had no family to take care of. Still, the memories of my mother (who was dead) and my father (happily living in jail), along with those of my ever self-sufficient aunt, passed quietly through my mind.

My father is a bit of an annoying subject, so I will first tell you the loving memories of my mother. I have heard at least that she stopped smoking during her pregnancy with me, so from this I've concluded that she must have loved me very much. I had never truly known her, except in the way that you know someone in whose womb you spent nine months. They say she died of cancer, but the fact that she died around, if not on, the day of my birth, left me with the strong impression that it was due to complications with my delivery. But I'm quite sure she must have loved me, just because I have thought about her every day I can remember. Somehow I knew that if she were alive, she would have made me a better person.

From the pictures I've seen, my mother was extremely beautiful. It's true that I've never seen any pictures of her from after she was hooked on cocaine, but that isn't something I've ever wanted to see anyway. It's completely understandable how my father fell in love with her, but how she fell for my father - and fell hard - I could never comprehend. My mother was stunning, with long black hair, big black eyes and dark black skin. Though she stood only five foot six inches, I am told she always commanded the attention of a room through the sheer power of her grace. I just know that she loved me.

My father's love however... Well, let's just say that I'm not as sure about that one. He is certainly an interesting character. He's someone who you wouldn't mind seeing on stage as a performer in a play, but not someone who you'd want to call father. He was always going to jail because of bounced checks. Lord knows that he had no reason to bounce checks as he made plenty of money from selling cocaine. I think, however, that he felt more secure in prison and for this reason kept a special bank account with no money in it, from which he would always try to draw thousands upon thousands of dollars.

It's not that my father isn't a smart man. On the contrary, he is extremely intelligent. He earned his Ph.D. in physics, but once he finished school he didn't seem to know what to do with himself. He had to find some excuse for hanging out on college campuses, as he loved to be around all of the young students. I think it was at this time that he started to sell cocaine and fell into a group that included my mother. I heard from my aunt that after the first time he was sent to jail for possession with the intent to sell, he found that he really liked prison. He mentioned to me once something about being able to relate to the people there. At any rate, he's called that place home for the better part of three decades so I don't imagine he can find it in himself to do anything else now. I certainly don't hold anything against him personally, other than the obvious distaste for selling drugs to kids, but I just didn't want to see or associate with him. We never became close as I was not at all into the prison visitation scene.

And then of course there was my Aunt Camille. She was not my real aunt mind you, but the courts recognized her. She was hospitable enough to let me live with her whenever my father went to jail, which as I said was pretty much all of the time. It meant relocating 500 miles south but it was worth it to live at my foul mouthed but ever compassionate, without love, as she would tell you, aunt's place. I actually believed that she was my real aunt up until our first fight when she informed me that she was no relative of mine, but as my father had done her some great service in his youth, she was obliged to return the favor. She would never tell me what favor he did for her, but she did allow me a spot on the couch and fed me a cooked meal every day, and I suppose that in this day and age you can't ask for much more.

Aunt Camille was in her early fifties when I first moved in with her. She really didn't want to have anything to do with me but felt that it was her duty to keep me alive. I wasn't allowed to have any friends over, but I wouldn't have wanted them to see my home anyway. It was comfortable enough for me, but I doubted if the kids from my school would have appreciated my pastimes, such as watching the cockroaches getting stuck in the roach motels or listening to that single Diana Ross album, the only album my aunt owned, for hours on end. And her shrieking voice that pierced my ears every time I looked in the wrong direction was something that only a nephew could love. But most disturbing was turning around and finding her pointing at me for no reason. She would always just stare and point at me with a look of utter contempt. Often as a kid, when I knew that I was doing something wrong, I would close my eyes for a second and this image of my aunt pointing at me would come clearly in my mind. I would usually awaken slowly in the mornings dreaming of her finger and then upon waking up find her standing above me with that evil index in my face. I couldn't begin to understand how fate could have allotted me such a place in life.

When I was young, I really didn't understand that I was poor, but I knew that I wasn't satisfied. Throughout my teenage years, I spent most of my time in movie theaters dreaming about other peoples' lives and wondering when fate would catch hold of me and turn my life into something meaningful. I was always the dreamer but never practical enough to put those dreams into motion. I was simply one of those people who always asked why but never how, and certainly never for what good reason. I just expected the universe to realize I was its center and eventually remember it needed to take care of me.

As soon as I'd graduated from high school, my Aunt Camille asked me to leave so she could sell her apartment and move into a retirement home. She lives there now, where I hear she has lots of boyfriends. She has an adequate retirement to live off of so she assured me that I had no responsibility to her, even asking me not to show my face at her center. She said that her duty to me was over and that my duty to her would be to move on with my life. I'm not sure if it was really my duty, but I did know that it was what would make her the happiest. She was old when I first met her and I knew she always resented having to put up with me -though I'm certainly grateful that she did.

Chapter 2

After about seven hours on the road I reached Sacramento. I'd originally planned on heading for San Francisco, the place of my birth, but as I neared northern California I decided to head east instead of west. I wanted to make a break from everything familiar to me, and so with complete abandon, I turned east onto Interstate 80, heading for the heart of America and leaving completely the comforts of my backyard.

As darkness fell, I found it increasingly hard to stay awake and had to slow down. My eyes focused solely on the white lines on the side of the road. I couldn't see anything in front of me due to the glare of oncoming traffic against my dirty windshield. I felt sorry for all of the motorists who must have thought that I was completely intoxicated as I kept following the line to the right at exits, quickly jerking the car back in line with the highway at the last moment.

I checked my watch and realized that I had been driving for more than fifteen hours. I stopped at a rest stop to freshen up and was shocked to see that my eyes were completely blood shot. This redness contrasted strikingly with my black skin, giving me a somewhat demonic look. My always neat and tightly braided cornrows -- I early on learned to braid myself, as my aunt wouldn't touch me, saying it was a liberty that would concede a closeness we didn't have -- were now messy with stray hairs sticking out all over due to my intense and continual scratching to stay awake. Seeing myself in this state, I became excited and headed back out with renewed vigor. I had never taxed my body this much before and this new experience, no matter how small, was energizing me.

At each new stop, the gas station clerks upon seeing my wild hair and blood shot eyes gave increasingly more concerned stares as I filled up on coffee and chips. My t-shirt and blue jeans were also stained with coffee and chocolate from lapses in alertness, which added to the overall look of insanity. Each time I saw the shock in the clerk's eyes, I was invigorated and good to go for another hour.

During the daytime it was easier for me to stay awake, but because of my drowsiness I was unable to keep up a fast speed and kept noticing that I was going slower than the speed limit. I didn't know what I would say if I was pulled over for going forty miles an hour, but I was pretty sure that the cop, after seeing me, would bring a halt to my plans.

As the second night passed I began creating new stretching positions to stay awake. No longer was this a pleasant ride but rather it was shifts of driving while tensing every muscle followed by stretching every tendon, followed by putting my head out the window and yelling into the wind, followed by parking alongside the highway and running up and down the street in order to freshen up. And then I would repeat the whole process over and over again.

At sunrise on the third morning I decided that if I weren't going to go to sleep at least I would take a break. I found a rest stop that had showers so I cleaned up, changed my clothes and went for a real breakfast. It was the first time I'd eaten anything besides coffee, chips or candy in two days. The scrambled eggs and hash browns were just what I needed. I stuffed up and felt as if I were starting a new day. I was ignoring the pounding in my head, which was a little easier now as my head was becoming somewhat numb.

My thoughts became crazy in the afternoon. I started to hear voices in my head that were not following any kind of logical pattern, but were rather like conversations in a crowd that you didn't pay attention to. I began to see different colored lights coming from the radio, which I was physically unable to hear anymore, though I imagine it was just playing static, as I had given up on changing the channel the day before. The other cars started to take on the shapes of animals and buildings. I remember one car even seemed to look like a grid on which I was struggling to solve a mathematical problem.

On the third night of my journey, after being on the road for more than sixty-three hours, I reached a point where I was stopping at every exit, getting out of the car, sprinting up and down the side of the road for about five minutes, and then getting back in the car to drive on to the next exit. I knew that my journey was proceeding at a snail's pace but I didn't want to go to sleep before reaching my destination. Not knowing my destination, however, made this more complicated. Eventually though, I could not bear the pain of staying awake any longer. My eyes felt like they were going to jump out of their sockets. My whole body was completely numb and my head was filled with visions of a hotel room. I didn't have any idea what city I was near or even what state I was in. Finally, coming to my senses for a brief moment of insight, I grasped the fact that I would soon be careening off the roadside. Realizing the inevitable, I took the next exit with the resolution of making that place my home. I pulled off the highway and looked in both directions. To the left there was complete darkness. To the right there was complete darkness. What was this? Where was the town? I knew I couldn't get back on the highway because there was no way I could make it to the next exit, so I just pulled along the side of the road and went to sleep.

Chapter 3

The first thing I noticed was the ringing in my head. I could feel my eyes trying to focus without the usual prerequisite of first opening them. My brain seemed submerged in a heavy fog, as I couldn't understand what it was that I was trying to do. Slowly, I became aware of my body, which felt numb all over. Then in one moment I felt a stinging rush of pain to my arms, while my bottom burned in it's squished position and my legs felt like dead weights, completely swollen from days of staying upright. I couldn't lift even a finger though I was trying to make myself wake up without yet knowing the reason why. Then, instantly, I remembered where I was, sleeping along the side of the road in my car, and I realized that there could possibly be someone watching me. With this sudden scare, the sounds of the outside world came rushing in. I could hear a tapping... No, it was a knocking... Quite a loud knocking... I fought with all my might to force my eyes open and finally with one hard push I sat straight up from my slumped position behind the wheel.

Again, I heard the knock on my window. Forcing my head to the left, I could barely see through my unfocused eyes, a kid standing there. As I struggled against the glare, I began to make out the figure of a young girl that was just standing still, staring at me. I wondered if she was scared, but she looked more as if she were waiting for me.

Unsure of what to do, I looked around and noticed that there was nothing in front of me but a road with grass on either side meandering into the horizon. Turning around, I saw the highway with the same road crossing over it and the same nothingness beside and beyond it. There were no houses or man-made structures, other than the road, as far as I could see. I began to think that maybe I was on someone's private farm property, but as I began to gather my wits I realized that there weren't even any farms around, just an endless expanse of grass.

As I gained some control over my body, I slowly got out of the car to fully take in the scenery. Every joint in my body rebelled against my movements and only with much pain could I stand up straight. The girl backed up about 20 feet, not scared but just keeping her distance.

"Where did you come from?" I asked her.

"I live here," she said with an annoyed shrivel of her nose. "I'm the one who should be asking *you* the questions, as I know I haven't seen you around here before." She acted much older than what I expected her to be although I could see she was trying hard to make me think she was very mature and in control of the situation.

"You live here?" Looking around I continued, "You live where?"

"Just down the road," she said, a bit irritated. "But where do *you* come from?"

"Just down *that* road," I shot back, looking down the highway with a smile. I had no idea how far I'd come, only that I hadn't yet fallen into the Atlantic, and was probably quite some distance from it due to my snail's pace.

"What's your name?" she asked.

"Ballard Davies. I'm from California."

"What? Ballard Davies?" she questioned. "What kind of name is that? It sounds more like the name of a store or a factory or something. Like 'Ballard and Davies Florists' or some such thing." She laughed for a moment at her own wit.

Used to the comments, I tried to ignore her. It was then that I noticed the weather was perfectly calm, no clouds, no breeze.

"Oh but you said you're from California, right? No wonder you have such a weird name. Ballard! Where did that come from?"

I had no intention of explaining my name to her.

"How *old* are you?" I asked, not really annoyed, but wanting to play along.

"Twelve."

"Do you know that I'm almost three times your age?" I lied, being myself only twenty-seven.

"So?"

"So, you're supposed to be a little more respectful to your elders." She was not impressed however, although she did try and loosen her face up a bit. She was a cute girl in her blue jeans and t-shirt and some old worn out sandals. She had long brown hair that fell in a single braid down to her waist, with strands hanging out and molding her slightly chubby face. Her big brown eyes seemed a bit fierce and mature though trapped in her kid's body.

"What's your name?" I asked her.

"Issa Philip-Stevens." She gave a special emphasis on the name Philip that made her seem especially proud of it. After a pause she asked, "So what *are* you doing here?"

"I'm looking for something to eat."

"You came all the way from California to find something to eat?" Her sarcastic face was back, although I did appreciate her wit. "I knew all you Californians were a bit weird. It's all that sun. Goes straight to your brain and fries it. You probably just came here on a whim and are just indulging your fantasies of freedom, or some such thing."

"Please. Is there a restaurant anywhere near here?" I didn't want to entertain her speculations as I felt they might be cutting too close to the truth and I wanted badly to stay positive about my adventure.

"Yes. There's a coffee house where you can get breakfast, just inside of town." She pointed north, down the road where she came from.

"Well, hop in and I'll take us there," I said motioning to the car.

"I don't know you."

"So?"

"So I don't get into cars with strangers and you are definitely strange."

"So how are we going to get there then?" I said with honest confusion.

"We can walk, of course." Now, I was definitely beginning to feel my aching bones in all their glory.

"We can't walk," I pleaded. "Besides, I'm not all that strange. I'm pretty normal actually."

"Let's see now... you came all the way from California to get something to eat. Your eyes are bloodshot and your hair's a mess... and you have a very peculiar name... Yes, I would definitely have to put you in the, 'too strange to get into a car with' category. Anyways, it's not very far, and you look like you could use the exercise."

I was not fat, though I had gained a little extra since my youth and was instantly taken in by her challenge. "Let's go."

I grabbed a toiletry bag and some clothes from my car and put them in a backpack, hoping that I would be able to clean up somewhere. And so we started on our journey towards the place I was determined to make my home.

The sun was up although it was not hot, the air was crisp and clean, and there was nothing at all to see. When I say nothing, I don't mean just the absence of cars or houses or other man-made structures, I mean *absolutely* nothing. There were no trees, no streams, no hills, and no bushes. There weren't even any clouds in the sky. I had never imagined such a place as this where nothing was. I had never been outside of California but I always imagined that Middle America would at least have cows roaming about the pastures. But this was something new. In California, open space like this would have been turned into a mall or modern housing complex by now.

At least I could be sure that my effort to start again would be successful as I imagined that there was no way, having grown up in these parts, I could have become the same person I'd become in California. Looking at Issa, I imagined that she must be so innocent and untainted by the "sins" of the city. I tried to imagine myself as a child growing up all over again here, while trying to push out all of the preconceptions that were already beginning to creep in about my new home.

Chapter 4

After about forty minutes of walking with no end in sight I began to suspect the worst. "Um, Issa, how far away is this town?"

"It's just up a ways."

"You said that an hour ago."

"It hasn't been an hour."

"But there doesn't seem to be any kind of living thing within sight of us."

"The grass is living isn't it? Some say that even the wind is living. But in answer to your question, the town is about six miles from where you parked so we've got about another hour and a half to go." My jaw dropped in amazement. She said it as if she didn't have a care in the world, but six miles I was unprepared for.

"How is it that you got all the way out here? Shouldn't you be in school or something?"

"My mom doesn't believe in the public school here so I get home schooling. Besides, school doesn't start this early in the morning." She shrugged her shoulders and kept on walking. After a second's pause I followed her. There could be no turning back now. If this was the way of my new home then I had better get used to it.

As I headed towards the town, I had so many high aspirations, although I knew that I didn't have much reason to be optimistic. I had about forty-five dollars in my pocket and that was it. I needed a job. I needed a place to stay. And I most definitely did not need another two hour walk back to my car at the end of the day! But somehow I felt free and that was better than any security that I had lost. I only hoped that the people of the town were as accepting as Issa.

"What is the name of this town, anyhow?"

"It's called Blue Bell."

"Blue Bell? That's kind of funny. What is it named after?"

"Well, *Ballard*... uh huh," she started with a smile. "About fifty years ago we had the name of Creekwood, but our creek dried up over a hundred years ago and we haven't ever had any woods in these parts. So we decided to rename the town after our oldest standing building. In the center of our downtown district is a clock tower and above the clocks are blue bells that ring every hour as many times as the hour." Her speech sounded rehearsed as if it was something that all the kids learned and remembered.

"You have bells ringing every hour? That must be kind of depressing. Isn't it like counting away the hours until you're dead, or something?"

Issa shrugged her shoulders and said, "My momma, Emma Philips, says that when times get hard the only thing that allows her to feel some relief is to think that one day she will be dead and it will all be over..."

"What will all be over?"

"I don't know... the endlessness of it all, I guess."

"The endlessness of it all?"

"Well, that's my momma's view anyhow, though my philosophies are much more complicated than that!"

"Your philosophies? My God! What does your mom teach in your classes? What grade are you in that you should have such profound philosophies?"

"I'm in seventh grade but I take tenth grade math!"

"Wow..."

"Yep."

I saw a house in the distance and assumed that the town was closer than Issa had said. Brilliantly, I pointed this out to her. Sadly I learned however, that this house marked the farthest reaches of the town. It belonged to an old widower who had gone batty since the death of his wife. He had moved out here to get as far away from the gossiping ninnies of the town as he could. As we neared his home, Issa quickened our pace to nearly a run but just as we were clearing his pathway we heard him yell, "Hey who's that there!"

"It's me, Issa, Mr. Landauer. And this is my friend Ballard." She said all this without stopping, not wanting him to come out and greet us.

"Well, what's Ballard doing out here this early? It's not even eight o'clock yet. Have the two of you had breakfast? Come on in and I'll cook some up for you. You walk on an empty stomach and you won't get very far." All I could see of him was his arm coming through an open window, gesturing vigorously for us to come in. His voice sounded very old and grainy, though he was able to yell pretty loud.

"Ballard has a meeting with Uncle Cheswick," she yelled. "Maybe tomorrow or the next day though!" She waved and smiled as we left.

"OK. Well, I'll see you then!" he called out after us.

"Who is Uncle Cheswick?" I asked Issa as we started to slow back down.

"He's not really related to me but all the kids call him uncle because he treats all of us as if we were his own. Anyways, he runs the coffee house where we're going, and you'll meet him, so it wasn't really a lie."

"Yeah, but now we'll have to come back here tomorrow because you said we'll show up."

"No, don't worry, I always say that. This is just habit and repetition for us. He doesn't remember from moment to moment let alone day to day; otherwise, he would have long ago given up on me. He's just a lonely old man. He has some kind of radar in his head because I can never pass by his house without him noticing me, and offering me breakfast. You know, I talked to him already once this morning when coming out here. We had real quality time. I said 'Hi' and he said 'Hi,' and then I said 'Bye' and he said 'Bye.' So you really shouldn't feel too bad, OK?"

I just shook my head and kept on walking.

"Don't worry," she continued, "if you really want to keep good on my word to someone that you've never met, then we'll go over there one day. And on that day you can do all the making up that you see fit, and after he realizes that you're just as crazy as he is then he'll go ahead and talk you into the ground."

"Great." I smiled.

"Well, that is if you stay here long enough. You're not planning on heading back to California tonight are you?"

"No, not tonight," I answered.

"So, how long *are* you planning on staying?"

"Forever, I think."

"*Forever*?"

"Well... we'll see."

"My God, you Californians really are strange!"

Chapter 5

After passing another seven houses spread out over three miles, we finally reached Issa's beloved "downtown district." The downtown consisted of one street running five blocks, east to west. The main feature and highest building, was a five-story, white-bricked clock tower with blue bells hanging inside the roof. There were clocks on all four sides of the building so as to be seen by all. In the distance, to the west, was the first hill I'd seen in this area and on it was spread a grouping of three buildings, which Issa told me were the local schools. About a half-mile north from there, raised up on a much larger hill, looking to me like a small mountain, and creating a valley effect for the downtown area, was a huge expanse of houses. The closer houses were small and modest but the farther they were up the hill the bigger the houses got, and in the distance the last of the houses were great mansions. In between their downtown and the houses were meadows, on some of which little parks were constructed, but mostly it was just open space. There was just one main road, the same road that we had walked on from the highway that connected the downtown to the school and then wrapped up the hill through the neighborhood, where it finally split up into many small roads creating the residential area. I was so happy to see the four to five hundred houses next to each other. I felt I was returning to civilization, although still wondering if I'd stepped back in time about fifty years. It wasn't so much that it was a small town, as I guessed there must have been a minimum of three to four thousand residents, but I wondered how they could all be supported by such a small commercial district, figuring they must go to neighboring cities to do any serious shopping.

Just as we entered the town, it turned 9:00 a.m. and the bells rang out nine times. There were three bells at three different pitches, which were struck one after the other giving them a very melodic and enchanting effect. But these bells were loud and it was somewhat scary to think that they were rung every hour. I'm sure they could be heard at the top of the hill where the last house rested, which made me wonder if anyone got any sleep at night.

To the west of the clock tower was a clothing store, and to the east of it was a supermarket. Next to the clothing store was John's Café, the resident get together coffee house, which at this present moment was half filled with old men having their morning coffee and reading the newspaper. As we walked in, I felt immensely conscious of the fact that, next to Issa, I was the youngest one there. Issa assured me though that it was only the time of day that brought out all of the old folks, and if I came back in the afternoon it would be filled with middle aged miners on their lunch break while at nighttime it would be stuffed to capacity with teens.

"Issa! Finally you've returned!" chided the half-bald, roly-poly man that seemed to be in charge there. "It's been five days girl! Five days! You know I can't survive without my daily fix of your smart little mouth."

"Yeah, I've been busy studying," answered Issa.

"I didn't expect you this early today though. What happened to your walk?"

"Well, I found some poor, hungry soul and I brought him to you." Issa pointed to me with a pathetic smile. "But you better be nice to him as I think he's not in the mood for any of your jokes right now. He's a little tired, and he drove a great distance just to have a bit of your famous pancakes."

"Of course I'll be nice to him," he said with a grin.

"Ballard Davies this is John-Walter Cheswick," Issa said motioning for me to step forward. I suddenly felt completely out of place, and unsure of how to act. I wasn't sure if I should be quiet at first or try and be as loud and jovial as he was.

"Nice to meet you, sir," I said, feeling a bit stupid with my old clothes and morning breath. Mr. Cheswick shook my hand vigorously as he looked me up and down with his grin. It was easy to see why the kids would call him uncle. He had a very rambunctious style and seemed the type that could put any stranger at ease.

"And it's nice to meet you, but you look like you could use a shower more than a meal! No offense, mind you. Just call it like I see it though, and right now I'm seeing someone who's in good need of some cleanin' up!" Mr. Cheswick's smile was wide, hidden only by his fluffy beard. He had more hair on his face than he did on his head, which was completely bald on top save for some scraggles rounding his ears and the bottom of his head. He was short and fat, and followed his every sentence with a moving back and forth of his hands. He wore a long white apron that almost reached the floor and was already dirty even though it was still early in the morning. In the pocket of his apron was a spatula. He had placed the spoon end of it inside the pocket, and the long handle sticking out kept poking him in the stomach. Although it was comical, I had to wonder if it was entirely sanitary. It was certainly endearing.

"Yes, I've been on the road for three days. I'm sorry for the appearance and, um, the smell."

"No need to be sorry for anything here! But we do have a bathroom and shower in the back so go ahead and put it to good use. Take your time and then come and get some breakfast."

"Well, if you're going to take a shower, then I'm going to be on my way," said Issa as she made her way to the door. "I have to start my homework soon, so I'll see you around."

"Thanks so much, Issa. I really appreciate it." I was sad to see her go. She was my one friend so far and I was mentally holding on to her as my security blanket. But I figured that in a city this small, it wouldn't be too long before I saw her again.

Mr. Cheswick slapped me on the back as he shooed me into the bathroom. I couldn't help feeling happy as I cleaned up, realizing that my first experience in this town was a friendly one. I showered and changed my clothes. I redid some of my braids so as to look a little more sleek and professional. Although I knew that first impressions were hard to shake, Mr. Cheswick didn't seem the type to care about any such thing. Coming out, I felt like a new man. Ready to start the day. Ready to conquer the world. Well, at least ready to have some breakfast.

Chapter 6

"Now you look ready to eat!" said Mr. Cheswick. "Just have a seat over there and Elizabeth will come and take your order."

I sat down and reviewed the menu while scanning all of the old men who were reading their papers and occasionally taking a peep at me. Behind the cooking counter, I saw the woman who was most probably my waitress, Elizabeth. She was thin, and had an extremely pleasant face. She had long, thick black hair that was mostly falling out of the bun she had put it in. Black lines around her eyes made her look as if she hadn't slept in quite some time. Those lines though, were rather like pools of blackness that spread out from her big brown eyes and was a stark contrast against her tan colored skin. It almost gave her the appearance of being a raccoon. She came over to my table and asked if she could take my order. Noticing that she had an accent, I asked her where she was from.

"Costa Rica." She said very dryly, seeming to make an effort not to smile or look me in the eyes.

"Costa Rica! Wow, how did you find your way over here?"

"We travel too..." she said, obviously annoyed. I thought myself exceedingly charming when I said it but she, I guess, didn't agree.

"So what would you like this morning?" she forced.

"Three eggs sunny side up, hash browns and a coffee... Thanks." Not seeming to care about my added thanks she turned around and walked away.

I watched her cook my food herself. She seemed to do everything in a very meticulous manner, not doing any extra actions, nor even looking from side to side or talking to anyone. She was completely concentrated on her task. I felt as if there was some kind of magic in the way she moved, as it seemed so purposeful. I was used to seeing cooks that didn't care about what they were doing, just trying to rush the needed things together while carrying on with some more important business like telling jokes to their friends. She was quickly finished and brought the items back to me.

Without raising her eyes to mine, she set the plate on my table. Then, pausing for a second, she said to me in a strong voice, "You don't even know me, so please don't look at me like you love me," and then walked away without so much as a glance or a nod. Needless to say, I was completely embarrassed. I had no idea that I was staring at her, or at least that she could see that I was staring at her. I felt bad thinking that she must get hit on a lot working in this kind of place and that the last thing she needed this morning was someone like me trying to make small talk. Unfortunately, her one line to me had the opposite effect as its intent. I was now completely drawn to her and couldn't help but keep knowledge of her movements out of the corner of my eye.

As I ate, pretending to look away from Elizabeth, I noticed a short, old, black man, the only other black man in the place beside myself, motioning for me to come join his table. There was a second man at his table, and they seemed to be together though the other man was not a part of this present distraction. Both appeared to be in their seventies. I didn't want to go over as I was still feeling the humiliation of my last conversation, but I knew that I had no choice. Unless I wanted to be flatly rude, I had to join his table. So, I picked up my plate, walked over and nervously sat down across from them.

"Hi, I'm Ballard." I figured that was as good a line as any, though I wished I could come up with something more original. Their faces also seemed to show some disappointment.

"I'm Ruben Bennet, and this is my brother in law Phiser Mitchell," said the one that had called me over, while Mr. Mitchell didn't bother to look up from his paper at the introduction. Mr. Mitchell's face was pasty white but covered with black lines and seemed to merge into the paper he was reading.

Mr. Bennet was very anxious to talk to me. His big, brown eyes were almost popping out of his face.

"What are you doing in this town, son?" asked Mr. Bennet. "Did you hope to find something here or are you just passing through? And I know that you're not just passing through since we are not in the direction of anywhere, so you must have come to find something."

Confused, I told him I hadn't lost anything. That I was just looking for a fresh start and this town seemed as good a place as any to make it. He was concentrating on my face as I talked and I wondered if he was trying to catch me in a lie. I began to wonder myself if I was lying and probably confused myself into looking as though I was making up a story when I was actually trying to be as honest as possible.

"Fresh start, huh? I've heard that quite a many times in my years, as I'm sure you can imagine. What is it that ails you, son? It doesn't appear to be the physical so it must be the mental... Or perhaps the spiritual?"

I didn't know how to respond to his questioning so I didn't say anything at all. Had I been back in my old home, I probably would have just laughed him off as a quack and walked away, but being here left me vulnerable and confused on how to respond.

"If it's the spiritual you're looking for, then this town can offer a few things," he continued. "But let me tell you that I can see some things that most people can't see. In your eyes I can see you're searching. The problem is you don't even know what you're searching for. And that, my friend can be the greatest problem we ever face. I can see you're lost. Do you dispute this at all?"

There was a pause and I realized I was supposed to talk now. Unfortunately, I had no idea what to say and so I just shrugged my shoulders and bowed my head down a bit, realizing that I was only giving a more pitiful and decidedly lost look as my answer.

"Better to answer kid, or he'll just keep talking," said the other man, Mr. Mitchell, without bothering to look up at me.

"The preachers down south where I'm from," continued Mr. Bennet, "used to tell us that what we needed was a return to Africa. I'm telling you, son that the concept was right but the method was most definitely wrong. As Africa is the motherland of humanity, a return there would be unifying. But, I'm not talking about the Africa of the world. No sir. It's not the Africa of the world at all. It's the Africa of the mind that we need to get to. If we ever hope to escape our suffering then we must return to this Africa of the mind." Mr. Bennet slowed his speech as if to ensure its comprehension. "We must return to the place in our minds where all was created and all is unified. I'm telling you, son, that spirituality is the only escape from the shackles of racism, sexism, humanism and selfism."

"Selfism?" asked Mr. Mitchell.

"Can you understand that?" asked Mr. Bennet, staring almost through me. "Can you?"

"Ruben, please. I can't even understand and I've heard that speech for the last forty years, so how do you expect *him* to understand?" Though I couldn't see Mr. Mitchell's eyes, his voice was very animated. He was slim and small with a black mustache that seemed out of place on his old, graying face.

I didn't have much to say but the two men soon finished their food and left me alone to finish mine. I was relieved that I didn't have to reveal my lack of knowledge about spirituality or African nationalism or mental creationism or whatever it was that he was talking about. The people here seemed so different from those at home, where I could sit all day in a restaurant and not have even one person look my way. Here, I had already made five acquaintances, although Elizabeth was perhaps already trying to forget me.

Eventually, Mr. Cheswick came back and asked how I was. I told him the food was exceptional of which he seemed quite proud.

"Well, can I do anything else for you today?" he asked.

"Uh, since you bring it up," I started slowly, "do you know anywhere in this town where I might look for a job? There doesn't seem to be many shops around here to pick from."

"No, you're right there. Most of the people here work out of town, some in the mines but most up around the university in Cloverdale. Actually, if you're not too concerned about the pay, the school on the hill there has been looking for a janitor for the past six months. Their last one just packed it up and left town one day. There's not too many people in this town that like that kind of work, as the kids can be a little messy."

"Oh, I don't mind that kind of work at all." Not really having done "that kind of work" before I didn't really know how I'd like it, but imagined that mining wasn't something I was ready to handle. More than this though, I felt that a job was a job, and if they were needy then I was ready to fill it.

"Then I would suggest that you just show up there around 3:30 this afternoon. That's when shift starts. Just show up and tell them you're ready to work and I'm sure they'll be ecstatic."

"Great! Thanks so much."

"Well, you can thank me after seeing your new work buddies, but no problem. No problem at all."

As I still had some time to waste before 3:30, I decided to make my way back to my car before it got any later. I knew that I wouldn't have the strength to walk back there after working my job, assuming of course that I got it, but I wasn't even sure if I had the strength to get back there now. The two hours it took me to get here would not go by so quickly getting back, without Issa as entertainment.

Chapter 7

As soon as I got out of Mr. Cheswick's café, I took off running and must have looked like a clown. Everyone's head turned to watch me, perhaps thinking that I had been spooked by some small town eccentricity. I was so excited, though, at the possibility of a job opportunity that I couldn't contain myself and wanted to get back to my car as soon as possible to privately revel in my good fortune. For the moment, all of the pain in my body had left and with the rush of adrenaline I was able to run a good mile before finally needing to slow to a walk to catch my breath. In my exuberance I found myself looking at the sky and smiling, while pumping my fist and muttering things such as, "Yeah, baby!" and "You better believe it!"

I would have made it back to my car at twice the speed it had taken to get to Blue Bell had I not fallen victim to an inbred politeness, brewed from the many years of pretending to appreciate the volatile verbal assaults of my Aunt Camille throughout my childhood. I was but two miles from reaching my car, and at present, my home, when I saw the crazy Mr. Landauer's house. It crossed my mind that I should start jogging again so as to look busy, but figured he wouldn't still be on the lookout. So I continued on with the same fast paced walk and just prayed that he wouldn't see me. I confidently told myself that since Issa wasn't here, he probably wouldn't even care who I was. Furthermore, he most likely only watched the street during the times he knew Issa would be taking her walk. This, though, was a false assumption. Just as I was passing the pathway to his front door, I heard the now familiar sound of his deep yet feeble voice calling out to me on the street. His front door was a good fifty yards from the roadside but he must have been on continuous watch, awaiting any passing visitors.

"Hey there!" came the voice. "I know you, don't I?"

At first I didn't see him, but as I scanned the house I saw a hand waving out of an open window. A second later his door swung open and he yelled to me, "Come in! Come in! You must be hungry!"

"No, I just ate lunch, actually." As it was now 12:30, I knew that it would take another forty minutes to get back to the car and I wanted to get to the schoolyard by 3:15. I was hoping to get a couple hours of sleep in before that to get the redness out of my eyes, as I wanted to be in my best form for my interview. So, I tried busily to think of what excuse I could offer to this man, forgetting temporarily the high ideals of truth and honor that I had expressed to Issa earlier.

Before I could say another word, however, Mr. Landauer came running down the pathway holding on to his long gray hair to keep it from flying around. When he reached me, he grabbed my hand before I was able to offer it and tried to shake it, though he didn't have much grip, so he just moved his arm up and down and it was up to me to follow the motion. "Well, you can at least have a cup of coffee. I'm in great want of a guest, as I don't get many visitors around these parts. It seems that nobody has time for old men these days."

Mr. Landauer stood awkwardly in front of me awaiting my answer, his long gray hair falling halfway down his backside. He was a little shorter than me, maybe 5 foot 7, and he looked up at me with his eyebrows raised in expectation. Although he must have been in his seventies, he looked like a child waiting for a gift. He smiled while tilting his head forward in a manner that seemed to be prying an answer out of me while his hands rested together on his small belly, shaking ever so slightly. He had on a thick gray sweater, though it was hot out, with a pair of long tan shorts that reached his knees. Covering his very thin legs were black knee-high socks and on his feet he wore black, slip-on dress shoes. Everything about him seemed to contradict itself. He seemed innocent, like a child, but way too old and knowing of the ways of the world to truly be. Seeing him standing before me like this, I couldn't help but accept his invitation.

"OK, but I don't have much time as I need to get back to town soon after picking my car up from down the road."

"Sure thing. Sure thing, my friend. What was your name again?"

"Ballard Davies, sir."

"Ah yes, Ballard. What a nice name that is. So, how have you been? How is your family doing? Are you feeling all right today?"

"Just fine," I answered as he escorted me into his home. The door opened up into a big living room that had paintings covering every inch of his walls of different men, women, boys and girls, that were enacting different scenes. There was very little furniture. The living room was completely bare, save for a card table and a small couch right in the center. There were four doors in the back of the room, and to the left there was a door standing open to the kitchen. He led me into the kitchen, where the walls were also decorated by countless paintings merging into each other. In the center of the kitchen he had three chairs and a table with polished china already set up as if he were expecting guests. On the kitchen counters, there were more plants than food items and they covered almost all of the space. The window above his sink had vines growing in from the outside and stretched up along his ceiling. I felt as though I were in a museum in the middle of the jungle.

"Did you paint these walls yourself?" I asked

"Ah, yes. This is the history of my family. I painted them when I first started to lose my memory, which did not go as far as people think it did. I had only begun to forget small things here and there, as it was a stressful time in my life. However, at the time I was not sure how far it would go, so I started painting all of my relatives on the walls so that I would never forget them. Most of them are no longer with me, of course. I shouldn't say 'of course' I guess, but it just happens to be the situation with me. At any rate, I am happy for their company in this form, since I don't get much of that around here. And they don't argue nearly so much like this; in fact I always put very pleasant words in their mouths."

"You're a very good painter," I said as if I knew anything about the subject.

"Well, thank you. It's the only hobby of a lonely man, though I'm starting to run out of space and am considering doing the ceilings next, but I think that might be too much strain on my back. Or, perhaps I could do the outside of the house, at least the backside. I don't want to fully cement my status as the town's most kooky resident."

"I'm sure there are plenty more kooky than you," I tried.

"Yes, to be sure, but a reputation is a hard thing to live down, and mine seems to be cemented in the minds of those around here."

Mr. Landauer heated up water for us in a tiny little kettle that didn't hold more than one cup of water at a time. This being the case, he heated up two cups one by one, and then mixed them together and separated them between the two of us, adding a lot of instant coffee, with a tiny amount of milk and sugar.

"You know," he said, "this is the first time that I've seen you walk with Issa. Have you known her long?"

"Actually, this is my first time coming here. I'm new in town."

"New?" A wide smile suddenly covered Mr. Landauer's face. "Well, how about that?" He seemed to be digesting the new information before continuing. "I'd better take this time, then, to tell you some things about myself, before the news gets to you through more menacing sources. Everyone in that town says I'm crazy, but I'm not. I just had a little breakdown after my wife died and I caused quite a commotion in town by running through the streets naked, yelling and breaking windows, et cetera, et cetera... Anyways, never quite getting over the embarrassment, I moved out here. Now I miss the people there, but love the land here, and am happy to stay here but would like more guests to come by. I try to get people to come over but it's hard for them to forget the memory of my last act in town. At least Issa comes by once a week and drops groceries off at my door, as I'm too old to walk into town for them. She is such a nice girl, but I'm afraid that she's also heard stories about me and so doesn't act completely freely around me."

"Really? I can't imagine Issa holding anything back from anyone. Though I certainly don't know her as well as you do."

"Nor do I know her as well as I'd like."

The old man was charming and quirky and I couldn't believe that anyone could hold a nervous breakdown against him. The coffee, unfortunately, was God-awful. It was like drinking mud. I drank slowly and deliberately, but could hardly swallow it by the end. I would let each sip rest in my mouth before deciding that there was no place for it to go but down. Eventually he commented on this.

"Do you not like coffee, Ballard?"

"No, I love it!"

"Because you're drinking it awfully slow, and your face, though I don't know your face well, your face seems a little pained."

"I'm not at all pained, just a little tired from my travels. Anyhow, I never take food or drink too fast in order to savor it." It seemed Issa was right. It was becoming too easy to lie to Mr. Landauer. I certainly wasn't doing it out of disrespect, but only to spare his feelings. Still, I was ashamed to be treating him like a child and figured he'd soon see through my lies. Instead though, he became suddenly inspired by what I'd said.

"You're so right, Ballard. So right, you know... For myself, I can say that my one true love in this world is coffee." He stopped for a moment gathering his words and straightening his posture. "It would seem that nothing soothes better, or is more comforting on a sad lonely day, than a strong cup of coffee. Sometimes I will just spend the whole day wallowing in self-pity, wondering what the purpose of my birth was, and then I pour myself a cup of coffee and it seems to gently whisper back to me, 'Yes my friend. I understand.'" Closing his eyes like a poet, he continued, "I have to say that it is so true that coffee is like the glue for this aching heart, and the counselor for this confused and weary soul. It is always there with open arms ready to embrace my every insecurity and say, 'You will always have a companion, shoulder and friend in me.' You know what I mean?"

I nodded my head eagerly in approval, but in truth I was completely speechless. Never before had I heard a more poetic homage to a beverage, and coming from this old man, whom for a moment looked as if he were going to cry, was too comical yet beautiful to describe. I too wanted to cry at this point, but for entirely different reasons.

"I like to drink coffee when I'm depressed also," I finally managed to say, but was ashamed at my lack of creativity. He also seemed less than thrilled as he got up and began washing the dishes. After he finished he again sat next to me and looked ready for a more serious discussion.

"You know, Ballard, your name is quite strange." His eyebrows were furrowed in a quizzical stare. "Where did it come from?"

I smiled at him, as was my habit when I was annoyed but not wanting to be rude. I slouched a little in my chair as I told him the story that I had told a hundred times before of why I had such a silly name. The story about how my mother was from Ballard, Washington. About how, when she went to school at San Francisco State University, she fell into a group that had two other women who shared her name of Maria. So wanting to distinguish her from the other girls they would call her Ballard Maria.

Eventually they began to just call her Ballard, a name that my father loved very much. When my mother died right after my birth, they decided to give me the name to remember her by.

"So they gave you a girl's name?" This was not the reaction that I was looking for, but I accepted it as it was said with such love from this old man.

"Well, it's not exactly a girl's name. It's the name of a town."

"Oh. So what's the town named after?"

"That's a good question. And you'd think that I'd have the answer but I don't."

"Fair enough. Fair enough."

"So your father must be sad you moved all the way out here then?"

"No, he's fine with it," was all I could muster. I didn't know Mr. Landauer well enough to be willing to indulge all of his questions, and I didn't feel in the mood to talk about my father right then.

We sat in silence for a couple of minutes before he jumped up and exclaimed that we had to play cards. He quickly ran out of the room before I could tell him I didn't have time, so I waited in the kitchen. After a minute he ran back into the room and saw me sitting there.

"We're all set up in the next room. I don't like to play cards in the kitchen, you know." He was tugging at my hand to follow him into the next room, which I did, to find that he had already dealt two hands on the card table.

"I'm so sorry Mr. Landauer, but I have to leave. I have a job interview to go to and I still have to pick up my car."

He looked at me with a sad, pathetic stare and I didn't know what to say. He also didn't offer any words or any outs. Eventually I forced, "I'll come by next week and play, though."

"Next week! I might not live till then."

Smiling I said, "Come on! You're not that old! But, ok I'll come back in a few days." With that he allowed me to leave.

I walked out of the house awkwardly, not wanting to run and show my happiness at being free but wanting to reach my car as quickly as possible. So, I walked fast, occasionally looking back to see Mr. Landauer watching me from the doorstep. Eventually the house was out of sight and at that point I broke into an all-out run. My heart was pounding and my mouth began to fill up with mucus but I didn't stop running until I'd reached my car. Unfortunately, after getting there I dropped to my knees and vomited. I'd forgotten how tired I was from three days of travel, and my sudden excitement and exertion was too much for my body to take, not to mention the fact I hadn't exercised in months and was simply running on the fumes of emotion.

Recovering, I moved my car a few feet from the mess I'd created and, having no water to rinse my mouth out with, I simply wiped it clean with a dirty shirt. I then set my watch alarm for 3:00, so as to get a one-hour power nap, before going to the job that would "change my life." Or at least fill it with something to do.

As I drifted into unconsciousness, I thought of the people I'd met so far. The image of the beautiful Elizabeth, and the one line I received from her, had left the most lasting impression on me. After about fifteen minutes of spinning her voice around in my head, my exhaustion finally took over and I fell asleep.

Chapter 8

When my alarm rang, the atmosphere had completely changed outside. Though the sky was clear, it had grown cold and the sun's effect could not be felt. There was a chill in the air that my car couldn't keep out and I felt as if my feet were starting to harden and freeze up. I got out of the car and jumped up and down a few times to wake myself up.

I was too excited about the possibility of finding work to be concerned with what kind of job I was going after. I knew that it would be manual labor, and while that wouldn't have been my first choice, I was not at all concerned about that now. I wanted badly to feel a part of something and to somehow join this community. I was sure that it didn't matter what I was doing as long as I was doing something. I felt the emotion of the moment well up inside of me, not knowing where it came from, but wanting to prove myself to whoever was giving me this opportunity. Physically, I felt strong and ready for any trial or test. In my mind I was making this into much more than a simple job, but rather an initiation into my new life, feeling that I had to be accepted at any cost; well at least any physical cost. So at 3:00, full of anticipation, I put on some nice pants and a button down shirt tucked in, drove into town and headed up towards the school.

I didn't have any idea where to go, so I just parked in the front parking lot and started walking alongside the three brick buildings. These two-story buildings stretched back in a straight row, one behind the other. The elementary school building was the closest to the entrance. I guessed that this was the elementary school, at any rate, because everything was on a miniature scale. The door handles were low, and looking in through the windows I could see that the tables were tiny. The middle school was next and I could smell the chemistry experiments coming through the windows, while the last building was for the high school. Unlike the first two buildings, the high school still had kids leaving from it, as the teenagers were all taking their time, in no hurry to say goodbye to their friends or their romantic counterparts. For a second, I indulged a few feelings of remorse that I wasn't still in high school, as it was such a carefree time, but then I remembered that my life in those days was not so carefree.

On the east side of the school there was a baseball field which all of the kids were filing out onto, and to the west was open countryside. About a half mile away on this western pasture I could see one single tree. This was the first tree I'd seen since getting off the highway. It was too far away to make out clearly, but it must have been quite big and quite old to be seen at all. I felt happy seeing this little spark of life and nature, which seemed so foreign in this town. I mentally committed to going out and visiting it as soon as I got the opportunity. The one thing my father always said he missed when he was in prison was trees. He said they were a source of strength, security and wisdom, which coincidentally were all of the things he was not in our relationship. I always wished he had chosen forestry rather than drugs as his career of choice, but that was now in a past that I was trying to forget.

I walked around the west side of the buildings. Behind the rear-most one I found a little shack with music coming from it. It was some kind of loud folk music, and I could hear the sound of feet stomping to the beat inside and loud voices talking, or rather yelling, amongst themselves. I could actually physically see the shack shaking from the vibration of the music. Outside of the building were a number of mop buckets and brooms lined up alongside large garbage cans with wheels on them. I figured that this must be the place and imagined what I was going to find inside. From the noise I supposed that there were probably about eight or nine young men dancing around, or at least having a good time.

When I walked in I was shocked at what I saw -- or could barely see. The room was completely filled with smoke, and there, in the middle of it, sat five men around a table playing cards. Well, I should say they *were* playing cards; they now all stared at me as if this were the first time such an interruption had occurred. The three men sitting together on the far side of the table all appeared to be in their sixties, and looked wide eyed and confused as they sat with their mouths wide open. The two on the near side of the table were younger, one middle-aged and the other seemingly about as old as me. This youngest one got up and turned off the radio, which sat in a windowsill. Then the middle-aged one got up, tilted his fedora hat back, took the cigarette from his mouth and asked how he could help me.

"Hi..." This got no answer but their stares. "Are you the janitors for the school?"

"Yeah," answered the young one.

"I was wondering if you needed a hand, or um, if you had a job for me." There was a moment's pause, which was then followed by loud laughter. The men nearly collapsed to the floor in surprise. They all started making funny faces at one another, mimicking their own previously shocked faces. I just stood there confused, waiting for them to fill me in on the joke.

As they all laughed, I struggled not to choke on the smoke. I didn't want them to think that I was weak or timid, so I just stood there as straight as possible, waiting for what was next.

The young one eventually walked over to me and said, "They were all afraid that you were catching us in the act of not working. They didn't know you wanted a job. They figured you were from the school board's office or something."

The middle-aged man then walked over to me and said, "My name's Lester. I'm the supervisor here. The young one is Ed, and those three numskulls, from the left, are Charley, Steven, and David." They really did look like a cast of characters. The three eldest of the group all wore matching blue overalls with white t-shirts and oversized black boots. Charley was clearly the oldest of them, with layers of bags under his eyes, but he sat very straight giving off a distinguished air. His gray hair was a complete mess of curls that fell into his face, with a long braid coming somewhere out of the shags stretching far down his back. He reminded me of some kind of great mad scientist, crazy yet completely in control. Steven's grays on the other hand were slicked completely back and his spine was curved enough for his elbows to rest easily on his knees. He had a couple of cuts on his face that appeared to be shaving accidents and his eyes were droopy, making him look half asleep. David wore a blue baseball cap, turned around backwards, and had a scruffy untrimmed beard that made him look a bit mean but his sarcastic smile eased the tension a bit. These three were clearly a group unto themselves, while the other two looked like add-ins.

Lester, the supervisor, wore a wide-brimmed hat that at the time I thought was to give a gangster effect, to add to the atmosphere of the card game, as it didn't match his blue jeans and sweatshirt. Later however, I learned that he always dressed this way, feeling that it gave him a managerial look. He also had a thin black mustache that didn't suit his face, and I couldn't help but feel that he was a bit of a dork.

Ed, on the other hand, was the epitome of cool. His curly black hair fell from beneath his baseball cap to his shoulders, not quite in the way of his eyes. He kept a well-trimmed five o'clock shadow and stood easy in his black jeans and gray T-shirt. He was slim, with a slight build to add to his chiseled face, giving him a 'Roman god-like' look. My clothes, on the other hand, would be the focus of their next amusement.

"Are you sure you came to work, man?" called out David not bothering to take the cigarette from his mouth.

"Yeah, you know, we don't play cards all day," was Charley's two cents.

Steven, in the middle of those two, just bobbed his head up and down. I would later find out that Steven was David's mute younger brother and only communicated by shaking his head as no one cared to learn the sign language that he tried to show them. It was hard for Steven to ever disagree or argue with anyone because no one ever took the time to understand his point of view, so he eventually settled on nodding his head 'yes' along with the comments that he most agreed with.

Steven, David and Charley had worked together for nearly forty years, having found nothing better to do after finishing high school. They liked the job because they could work together and Charley especially loved to read the books. Though they were only grade school level, he spent half of his time reading through the science and mathematics texts. He would even lecture the janitors about how math was the highest unchangeable truth, worthy of worship by all men. And the pursuits of science, he felt, were the most enjoyable and enlightening pastime for an educated man -- next to cards of course.

"Are you coming from the city or something?" asked Lester sarcastically, with a laugh.

"Yep! Definitely from the city!" affirmed David. "Probably somewhere out west. Maybe California or somewhere posh!"

"Yes," was my only answer, confused as I was.

"Well, we wear jeans out here in Blue Bell," continued Lester. "Those slacks are going to get tore up. And the wax-stripper we use on the floor will eat right through those loafers of yours."

"Yeah, we clean computers my friend, not type on them," added David as they all laughed. I just stood there with my dumb smile trying not to say anything stupid and wondering how I was going to fit in with these guys.

Ed brought me some rubber boots and said, "At any rate we could use the help 'cause it means more time for cards. You'd better clock in."

"By the way... How much does it pay?" I inquired with some hesitation.

"It's \$6.60 per hour and you get paid every two weeks. The work is hard but it gets over in about six hours so that leaves two hours for cards." Lester, I couldn't help noticing, seemed quite proud of the fact that he was the supervisor. I, though, wondered how I was going to last two weeks on my remaining thirty-two dollars.

"So, now that we've got six again we can go back to like before. Charley and me will take the grade school. Steven and David can have the middle school and Ed and... and..."

"Ballard Davies," I told.

"Ed and *Ballard Davies* can clean the high school." Lester finished his speech and took up a broom like it was his weapon to go to war with. "So we'll meet back here at 9:30. Let's get to it."

Ed gave me a time card to fill out and clock in and explained that our next pay day was in one week, but that we only get paid for the previous two weeks' card. So I actually wouldn't be getting paid for three weeks and that it would only be one week's worth of pay. Dejected, I planned my rations for the next three weeks. If I spent one dollar a day I could last. I figured that I would have to live on candy bars, that being the cheapest food I could think of.

Ed was very friendly. As we worked cleaning tables and sweeping and mopping floors, he told me about his family. His father was a clerk in the mayor's office and his mother taught ballet to young girls. He had lived in this town all his life and hadn't gone further than the reservoir, about 20 miles down the highway. And that had been a great event. He had traveled in the back of a truck with two other families and they had had a picnic and stared at the water and played cards. His main love, though, was playing his guitar, which he spent the better part of every day doing. Such simple pleasures, it seemed, would be a staple of my new life!

Ed explained that he'd been working with this gang ever since graduating high school about ten years ago. His father was hoping that he would go to college and study politics, promising to get him work in the local bureaucracy, but working behind a desk, or in public office, held no interest for him. He loved to argue politics but was not big on action. His mother, knowing that his heart was in music, had hoped he would at least study that in college. Ed though, felt that only natural musicians ever made it anyway, and that there was nothing much to learn in school, so he opted on becoming a janitor where at least he would have some level of freedom.

The work wasn't too hard, just a little tedious, since the kids made a lot of little messes here and there. Ed mostly stressed working fast over doing a good job, which immediately put me at ease, as I figured there must not be anyone overseeing the quality of our work.

At around 9:30, Ed and I rejoined the others in the shack, or what they called the "little laundry room" (as there was a washer and dryer for us to wash our rags and mops in). Since I was the newest member, I became the laundryman and coffee maker, so I started a load of wash, brought everyone a fresh cup of joe and then sat down for a game of cards.

"What game do you play?" I asked.

"Poker! What else?" was David's indignant response.

"Um... I don't really know poker."

They all looked at me as if I were extremely dumb. I felt even stupider than the kid who had left his muffin on the floor for a hundred other kids to walk over and had received countless mental curses from me that night.

"Well, what game do you know?" asked Ed.

"I know 21 and I know Speed, but that's only for two people."

"Listen here. You start out with five cards," began Charley in an extra gruff voice, as he taught me the ins and outs of poker. He told me when to fold and when to look as if I was thinking about folding and when to act as if I had a great hand.

So, slowly we passed away our remaining two hours of work. I spent that time feeling more stupid than ever as I lost game after game after game. But the last five minutes of the night I started to see the cards a little more clearly and hoped that tomorrow might be a better day. They bet with chips and in the end Charley came out on top. I was anxious to see what the winner got as I had no money to back up the chips. I was glad to find that the winner only received a handshake and a "well done."

When the clock struck twelve and the blue bells rang twelve times, we packed up, clocked the time cards and walked out into the pleasant night air. The town was completely dark and shut down. The stars were brilliantly shining due to the lack of city lights. Saying our goodbyes as we went, we all got into our cars and drove away. I imagined them returning to their happy families, who would certainly be asleep already, but at least they wouldn't be alone, while I sadly went back to my desolate spot beside the highway.

After reaching my parking space I got out of my car and looked up at the night sky that covered the entire expanse from horizon to horizon. Looking up, I wondered how I could have ever felt that I was somehow special and entitled to some privilege that isn't meant for everybody. For in this moment, I felt I was such a small and unimportant part of this vast universe. I wondered how it was that any of us could ever feel important when we were obviously so minute in the scheme of things. As I searched my mind for something to give me strength and comfort in this new life, I eventually settled on the face of Elizabeth. It was true that it was just the beautiful face of a girl I didn't know, but in this moment I just needed some image to cling onto and hold for the sake of feeling secure in my new environment. I thanked God for at least giving me something to do with myself and got in my car to end the day, not wanting to be awake any longer.

Chapter 9

The next week would pass very slowly for me. During this period of my life I developed a hefty appreciation for time. Time must be such a patient fellow to put up with the monotony of each moment. Each second ticking away with ungodly precision, reminding itself that it cannot escape its own perfection. And those wretched blue bells were like a pain in my side. I waited and waited for their ring and then I cursed them when they finally came and did not sing the number of rings that would signify the end to my struggles. Each second was like a weight being added to my shoulders, asking me why I had left comfort for starvation, certainty for uncertainty, security for freedom.

My only salvation, if you can call it that, was my job, which if nothing else, filled out a portion of the day. The work itself was relatively easy but there were other inherent problems that I hadn't counted on. The most difficult part was the psychological effects that different rooms had on me. I didn't find cleaning the classrooms to be any problem as I was glad to be out of school, but when we would clean the teacher's offices I would feel sad. I had long ago dreamt of being a university professor. Of which subject I didn't know, though I always liked history and psychology. But I had never planned on being a janitor. As I wiped down their computers, I would think that I was supposed to be the one sitting in front of the screen. As I emptied their trash, I would think that I was supposed to be the one making the mess. I didn't know where my grandiose ideas of my own significance came from but this job was beginning to give my ego some puncture wounds. I began to take every drop of spilled coffee as a personal insult to my manhood. And every handprint that I had to wipe off of the glass doors became an opportunity for me to curse the child or teacher who did not have enough sense to use the handle.

It was still two more weeks before I would be paid and, as expected, I was forced to live off of one candy bar each day, which I got from the vending machine at work. The others all ate their dinners together. They'd always tell me that I should bring something to work as eight hours was too long to go without eating, explaining that it was even worse because we were working. Every night I gave them the same answer, saying that I didn't eat at night, which they readily accepted before digging into their own meals. They didn't seem to notice the fact that I had lost ten pounds in less than ten days. Nor did they notice the bags that were forming around my eyes, which I didn't feel I deserved since I slept for the better part of most days, albeit sweating away in my car.

While awake, my hunger began to completely overtake me. I was eating the remains of sandwiches left in garbage cans or the jellybeans and muffins I found on the floor of the school. On one especially pitiful night I even warmed up half a cup of noodles that I found on the table in the teacher's lounge -- and I admit to you that those noodles were delicious! Still, I never would have dreamt I could have come down to this level, but hunger took over my mind like a fierce intruder unable to be brought under control. My only thought was that in a couple more weeks I would get my first check. And while it wouldn't be enough to rent a room, it would be enough to feed my stomach.

The others at work never asked about my home, or what I did with my time. Ed talked to me the most, and he knew all the local gossip. I knew everything that went on in the Mayor's office. I knew who was sleeping with whose secretary, and who fell in love with whose wife. He took special joy in telling me the failings of the other janitors. Things such as Lester having left his wife and child for a younger woman who seems to hate him, or how David always hits Steven in the head when he thinks that no one's looking.

Ed seemed to have a special love for Steven, which I figured was because he was a mute and wasn't able to yet work his way into Ed's bad book. He told that Steven was much smarter than people gave him credit for and that if you looked into his eyes you could see that he had so much to say. Because he was mute, people took him for stupid, but the real imbecile, in Ed's opinion, was Lester. He never was sure when talking with Lester if they were having the same conversation. He liked to say that Lester was big on talking but horrible in actual communication. Though Lester was stupid, that was much better than David, who was just a mean old man. It was funny to hear Ed say that David always had something negative to say. But unlike Ed, who had his share of charisma, David would deliver whatever he said in the harshest manner possible so as to put everyone else around him down and keep himself up on a pedestal.

Charley also kept himself on a pedestal but Ed thought that it was maybe more deserved. Charley was the most educated of them and the most interested in education. He looked upon himself as the one to lead the other janitors out of the darkness, and Ed admitted that Charley was probably the only one who could do the job.

Though he was such a gossip, Ed had a certain charm about him that made people want to be his friend. His features were very handsome, but more than that he always acted confident and at ease. As much as we talked though, I never told him about my own condition. I knew he would be interested in my life but was first waiting for me to open up to him. I didn't want him to have pity on me though, and I didn't want to become a burden on his life, so for those reasons I didn't reveal too much to him. Unfortunately, this hiding left me feeling alone. I realized that my condition was much worse than what I'd suffered in California because, though I was alone in San Diego, I was not starving. At the same time, if it didn't work out here I might as well starve, as there was certainly nowhere else to go.

Chapter 10

My melancholy began to lessen during the second week as my stomach began to shrink and the pangs of hunger were not quite as noticeable as before. So far as I didn't think about food, I didn't have a problem. Not to say that I stopped eating from the garbage, but at least it freed up mental time for thinking about other things. It was at this time that I remembered one morning upon waking up that I did indeed have a friend in this town. That I already knew of someone who was willing to feed me in return for only my lousy company. More than this, it was someone whom I'd promised to pay a visit to within a few days but had neglected. Good old Mr. Landauer. He would surely feed me without my asking and I would just have to put up with that awful coffee of his, which at least was better than no coffee at all.

So at 10:00 a.m. I drove up to his house, and before I even reached the door heard the most pleasant call of, "Ballard, Ballard, my good friend. It's so nice to see you again." What a difference a week makes. His gruffly voice now seemed to be so beautiful. Waving his arms here and there, he welcomed me as if I were a long lost relative. And I was, at least, most definitely lost.

I was embarrassed to be entering his house under these circumstances and found it hard to look him in the eye. All I could manage to say was, "Do you want to play cards?"

"Cards? Of course... Anytime," he said with a hesitant smile, not yet sure what to make of me. And then, after a second, after sensing my condition, he went into full-on host mode. "Come on in and sit down, my friend. Would you like some coffee? Here let me make some coffee for you. Would you like some crackers? You're looking kind of thin... Would you like some peanut butter to go with those crackers?" Mr. Landauer was watching me closely as if he only needed to see my facial expressions, which he mirrored on his own face, to understand what was going on with me. I was trying so hard to eat slow and not show my excitement but from his face I knew that he saw my whole condition.

"So, how's it going in town?" he asked, as he pulled out some bread and started making cheese sandwiches.

"Oh it's great. I got a nice job. Forty hours a week... Cleaning the school. And the people there are pretty nice." I was trying hard to smile but this was creating what must've been painfully funny expressions. I could only lift half my mouth into a smile, and kept thinking to myself, "lift the other half you stupid fellow!" But I was too nervous to gain control over myself, as I felt that I was here under false pretenses and disgracing both Mr. Landauer and myself in the process.

"Cleaning the school? Well, it's good for a start. So where are you staying?"

I hesitated to answer, not wanting to seem in a completely pitiful state. But there was no hiding that my clothes were old and that I hadn't been able to reach all parts of my body in my daily bath in the gas station sink. "Just down the road," I said.

"Down the road there..." he pointed. "Oh... You mean like a *MAN* under the *STARS!*" he said in a boisterous voice, puffing out his chest to play on my pride.

"Yeah, something like that," I laughed, though I really wanted to cry. On my first visit to this house, Mr. Landauer seemed so childlike and needy, but now that I needed something from him he suddenly appeared to be my only hope and friend. I felt horrible that I had thought anything bad about him and was now looking to him for help.

"Well, do you need a place to stay? Because I could give you a room to rent for, say, $250.00 per month, or if that's not possible then we could work out some sort of barter agreement. And if that's not possible you could stay for free even. Because this is a big house, you know, and it's in definite need of some other inhabitants. Well, what do you think?"

I could not believe my ears. He was telling me more than I could have ever hoped to hear. "I don't get paid for another two weeks, but I could make the rent up in a month. I would definitely love to stay here with you, that would be so great." I was talking so fast that my mouth could barely form the words before I spit them out.

"Even if you need two months to get yourself financially settled, it's no problem. I'm dying for the company and you need a shower so it works out for both of us." He smiled from ear to ear and patted me on the shoulder.

I was ecstatic to say the least. When I finished eating I washed my clothes, took a shower, and then played cards for a couple of hours with Mr. Landauer, before leaving for work. I felt twenty pounds lighter as the weight of desperation had been lifted from my shoulders, and the pain of starvation relieved from my stomach.

That night at work I was unusually happy and cordial with all. I actually sang my entrance, "How do you all do? 'Cause I'm doing fine!" and they obviously couldn't help but notice my change. Upon finding out the reason for my newfound humor though, they began scolding me incessantly for not revealing my plight to them earlier. Their yelling at me however, only made me feel even more happy, as I felt that someone actually loved me enough to be this concerned for me. They were quite surprised to hear about Mr. Landauer for it had been a long time since they'd even heard his name.

"My God! Is that old man still alive!" exclaimed Lester. "I'd heard he was trekking through the Cascades, or some such thing, and figured he'd done froze to death by now."

"Are you kidding, man?" said David. "Men like Mr. Landauer don't go so easily. They live merely to show you that they are indeed still alive despite all of your prayers that it should be otherwise." This was followed by a disapproving twitch from his younger brother.

"After all he's been through, you'd think he'd want to die," added Lester. "The sheer humiliation of his life, for me, would be too much to bear."

"What, you think your life is not humiliating to us?" offered Ed with some contempt, leading to chuckles from the others.

"Huh? This coming from the rock star?" asked Lester. "I shudder to think who would care."

"But seriously, Ballard, if there was ever a more arrogant and self-righteous man than Mr. Landauer, I don't think I've ever met him," said Charley. "His own family disowned him. I don't know how you will put up with all his preaching and questioning and trying to remind everyone that God has shined his special light on him." Charley slowly shook his head in memory of some past events. "Even I used to love the man, the speeches he used to give, but..."

"No, no. You are completely mistaken. I don't know anything about what you guys are saying, but there's certainly nothing self-righteous about Mr. Landauer. In fact, he is one of the sweetest men you could ever hope to meet. He's not arrogant at all. He listens to everything that you have to say and is interested in all your problems. You must be thinking of somebody else, or else he has changed drastically since you last met up with him." I was sure that they were only under the sway of years of gossip produced by Mr. Landauer's unfortunate breakdown when his wife died. They had many misconceptions of him, and I had no problem in singing his glories and trying my best to dispel their notions.

"You should have told me sooner though," said Ed. "It would have been fine for you to stay with me until you got yourself together."

"I know, but I didn't want to impose on you."

"Yeah some people just like to suffer," offered Lester, which drew an irritated look from Ed.

"You all are young still and haven't learned the first thing about suffering," said David. "Don't worry, you'll suffer much greater things than starvation before it's all said and done."

"Why think of it as suffering?" offered Charley as he got his work supplies together. "Believe me, there's no greater teacher in this world than misery."

As I stood shocked at his words, he sat down at the table in front of me and took out a pair of glasses from his pocket, glasses that I didn't even know he had, put them on and looked straight at me. He suddenly looked like a professor as he continued talking.

"I repeat, in case you missed it, that there is no greater teacher in this world than misery. It gives you character and respectability if you take from it all that it has to offer. A real friend would point out all your faults, but how many true friends do we have in this world? One if we're lucky. But misery is a friend that we can always count on. It teaches self-control and helps us to distinguish between right, wrong and necessary. It helps us to contemplate the meaning of life, and if we are unable to find that meaning, it helps us to deal with it. The best advice that I could give you, Ballard, is to not be afraid to befriend misery, because it will haunt and torment you until you do."

Confused as to how Mr. Landauer's best friend was coffee and Charley's was misery, I just laughed and told him that I would be happy just to be free from my endless mood swings.

"Free?" Charley asked with a sly smile. "Till death or contentment, whichever comes first, misery will see to that. Free eventually yes, but you must choose the path."

Chapter 11

The next couple of months passed in relative peace as I began to feel that I was actually starting to live a normal life again; normal, at least, in the sense that I had a routine that didn't involve sleeping while freezing in my car, or eating from the wastebaskets at work. It was the little pleasures though, that we usually don't appreciate, which gave me the most joy. Things such as washing my clothes in something other than a sink, suddenly felt like indulgences that kept me smiling. Just pulling up to Mr. Landauer's house every night and thinking to myself that this was my home and inside there was a warm bed waiting for me to curl up in, gave me goose bumps. And Mr. Landauer's quirky yet always insightful conversation made me feel as if there was someone in my life who really appreciated me. This was probably the greatest thing for me, as growing up I had never before lived with someone who had actually wanted my company. I had no mother, whom I constantly thought of, and a father whom I fought to forget; not to mention an aunt who wished she could forget me. But this new figure in my life, like a loving grandfather, gave me immeasurable joy.

Within two months, I paid Mr. Landauer all of the money owed him and had spending change in my pocket. Groceries were never a problem as the little girl, Issa, though I never saw her, dropped a bag of food off at the house early every Monday morning. Eager to pull my own weight though, I supplemented her food with more exotic items such as fruits, potatoes and hot chocolate, which were never a part of her supply. Mr. Landauer was used to living on a simple diet of rice, black beans, cheese, and coffee. I, on the other hand, was not yet ready for this kind of ascetic life, and he accepted and encouraged whatever changes I brought to the house.

Issa was somewhat of a mystery, as Mr. Landauer wouldn't talk about her, though I had badly wanted to see her again. She was one of those few friends I made on my first day here. I was somewhat surprised that she never came to visit me but figured that there was no reason she would know I was living there as she probably never talked with Mr. Landauer and didn't attend the school where I worked. Though I had prodded him about Issa many times, Mr. Landauer always shied away from talking about her, giving me the impression that she was somehow a part of his past that he was either ashamed of or that was just too painful to discuss. He always seemed to have some urgent business to attend to in his room whenever the subject of Issa or her family came up. I suspected that Issa was part of some community outreach program that Mr. Landauer was embarrassed to be on the receiving end of. I contented myself in my speculations, hoping to one-day meet up with her again.

Remembering the café where Issa first took me, I figured that I could probably find out information about her there. But, I shouldn't say this was the only or even the most pressing reason why I decided to make my way back to that place. A second reason was that I wanted to show Mr. Cheswick that I had made something of his advice. But even more than this, the real reason that I wanted to return to John's Café was that there was an image that hadn't left my mind since coming to this town -- and I wanted to see her face again even if she still wouldn't talk to me.

After two months, Elizabeth was still haunting my thoughts. I couldn't seem to escape her sad beauty. I hadn't wanted to see her again until I was able to talk with her on an equal footing, or at the very least, to not be the same pathetic, garbage eating, stinker that I had become for a short time. Still, on my last visit I wasn't able to say anything that she didn't take offense to, so I didn't know how I could fare any better on this occasion. I was never very smooth at talking to girls that I was interested in so it was slightly funny that I was thinking of pursuing someone who wasn't at all interested in me. But I felt as if there was a magical pull, no matter how stupid it sounds, and decided to see where my instincts would lead me.

When I pulled up outside of the café, I saw that the two old men, Ruben Bennet, and Phiser Mitchell, from my first day's visit, were just walking out. It was the first time that I was actually seeing Mr. Mitchell's full face without the aid of his newspaper. Mr. Bennet's face however, would have been hard to forget as he had drilled me with questions that even now were causing me to suddenly tense up. Thinking of how awkward that first visit was, I decided to hide in my car until they had passed me by. Unfortunately, they saw me watching them and, noticing me, their faces both brightened up as they walked straight over to my car. I quickly got out in order to greet them properly, but I could see that they clearly knew I had planned on letting them pass unnoticed.

"Ballard! It's nice to see that you're still around." I believe these were the first words Phiser Mitchell had said directly to me, and was shocked that he even knew my name.

"So, you stayed," started Mr. Bennet. "Does that mean you've found what you're looking for? From your eyes I'd guess you're still confused and I'd be willing to bet that you've not thought about what I told you even once."

"No, I remember," I chimed in stupidly. "You told me about spirituality and Africa, and the motherland, and um, racism."

"Oh no," said Mr. Mitchell. "Last time you were at least smart enough to keep your mouth shut, but Ruben isn't going to take kindly to this."

"No Phiser. I'm OK," said Mr. Bennet slowly. "He is a young one and I can't expect it all to sink in at once."

"Maybe he doesn't care," prodded Mr. Mitchell.

"No, I care! I care!" I suddenly exclaimed, not even knowing what it was that I thought I cared about.

"You're right Phiser, that he probably doesn't care. As even you don't care."

"That I don't, Ruben." It was all a game to Mr. Mitchell.

"But someday he will be forced to confront the truth of the mind and on that day he will remember my words. Return to the motherland, my boy! The motherland of the mind!"

Mr. Mitchell just laughed as the two walked away with their papers under their arms. I was now completely unsettled as I walked into the restaurant. Mr. Cheswick instantly recognized me and stopped what he was doing to hurry over to greet me. He almost knocked me over as he slapped me on the back and I couldn't believe that he was this happy to see someone he had only met once before.

"Hey! Ballard, isn't it?"

"Hi, Mr. Cheswick. It's so nice to see you again." I was now very unsure of what to say, as I didn't want to bring any more offense to anybody.

"My God, boy. Where have you been? I thought you'd passed on by, as I hadn't seen you since that first day. But Issa had mentioned something about you the other day so I knew you must be around somewhere."

"Issa?" I asked, somewhat surprised that she knew I was still here.

"Yeah, you remember the little girl that-"

"Of course I remember her. I just hadn't seen her since then and didn't know that she knew I was still alive. Is she here? Or is she coming later?" I asked.

"No she usually comes in earlier than this, though you can't set your clock by it. She pretty much sets her own schedule."

"Yeah, she seemed pretty independent."

"That she is. Gets it entirely from her mother too." Mr. Cheswick led me over to one of the booths and we sat down as if we were having a family get together. I was slightly unnerved by his boisterous display of affection, thinking that he would be drawing attention from the other customers. I was wanting to be as anonymous as possible after suffering humiliation moments before with Ruben, but apparently the other customers were used to this as no one seemed to even lift their eyes to look at us.

"Issa is definitely one of the best though," continued Mr. Cheswick.

"I'd really like to see her again sometime," I added.

"Oh, don't worry. You can't help but run across her, or trip over her, if you stay here long enough. She's all over the place." Mr. Cheswick seemed to be in an especially good mood as he took off his apron and settled into his chair as if he was planning on having a long talk with me. He still had his spatula in his hand though, and waved it slightly as he continued to talk.

"Speaking of sticking around... did you get the job at the school? I'd heard they hired someone but wasn't sure if it was you as I hadn't seen your face for so long."

"Yeah, I got the job. You were right, all I had to do was walk in and they were more than happy to hire me. Plus they are such an unusual cast of characters that it always makes going to work an interesting experience."

"And how's that Edward doing? I haven't seen him around for a while. Is he staying out of trouble? He's quite the rowdy."

"Who? Ed? Yeah, he's great." I found the question curious, as I never imagined Ed as someone who got in trouble or was at all rowdy. He always seemed laid back and rather smooth to me.

"I agree, he's great, just don't get too close. Some people are fun to hang out with as long as you steer clear of their influence, while others make great friends and will never consciously lead you astray. He is definitely the first type."

I couldn't in any way comprehend what Mr. Cheswick was saying. How could this man who seemingly didn't have a bad word for anyone else, give a warning about my work partner who was the one who was giving me the ins and outs of this small town life? Surely Ed would never intentionally lead *me* astray.

"Don't get me wrong," continued Mr. Cheswick, "I love Edward. We've been friends for a lot of years. Just don't get too close, that's all."

After a few seconds of silence, marked only by Mr. Cheswick's smile, he suddenly seemed to realize that I might have come here for reasons other than catching up and asked me, "So what can I get for you today?"

"Could I just have a cup of hot chocolate?"

"Certainly."

I was surprised that he was the one taking my order and looked around the room for Elizabeth, but she was nowhere in sight. He must have read my mind, because, without my asking, he said, "She goes to the university in Cloverdale on Mondays and Wednesdays."

Shocked, I tried to play it cool.

"Who's that, sir?" I knew that I was being stupid but it was too late. I could see that I didn't fool him in the slightest but he went along with my game anyway.

"Oh, Elizabeth," he said with a smile. "She's the girl that is usually working here with me."

"Oh yes, I remember her. That's nice. What is she studying?"

"Psychology."

"Psychology?"

"Yep. She's quite a bright one, all right."

"That's great. So is she going to become a therapist? I guess she doesn't want to be a waitress all her life."

"No, nor would I let her get stuck at this job. Not that I don't love her here and love this job myself, but I want her to move on and do what she loves."

"What does she love?"

"She really loves helping people. That's her nature. What she wants to do is work with kids doing some kind of job that will benefit them. Maybe start an after school center or some kind of community service program." Mr. Cheswick was very proud of her, almost like a father, though they didn't seem to be related. However, I didn't feel that it was my place to ask their exact relationship.

"So, what about you Ballard? What are your plans?" Mr. Cheswick had not yet gone to get my hot chocolate but his questions made me suddenly thirsty as I was not one with an interesting past or planned future, nor did I presently want to think about such things.

"Well, right now I'm just trying to get a stable footing here in Blue Bells."

"What about school? How far did you complete in school?"

"I did a couple years of college."

"A couple," he said with a laugh. "Decided it wasn't for you, huh? Yeah, me too. I figured why spend money when I can make it!"

"Well, it wasn't exactly like that. I just needed a break and didn't really know what I wanted to study. I didn't really have any plans, and I already had a decent job cashiering at a nice bookstore."

"Huh. I guess it wasn't that nice, since you left it."

"I left for more personal reasons."

"Personal reasons?"

"Well... I just wanted to see what else life had to offer. I wanted to leave the city and find something more real." Now I felt pretty stupid. How could life be less or more real? Did I even know what I was saying? I just wanted to run and hide but there was nowhere to go, and Mr. Cheswick's big, smiling eyes were smothering me. I told myself to sit up straight and pretend that I wasn't being as silly as I thought I was, but I kept slouching more and more close to the table, hoping to eventually find myself under it and away from those prying eyes.

"Well, nothing is quite as real as starving, huh?" He laughed as he said this and I knew that it was all just a joke to him, but to me it was much more than that. It was true that I had no idea what I was doing with my life, and that being the case I had no business trying to drag any girl into it.

Mr. Cheswick finally brought my hot chocolate, which I struggled to finish as my throat was suddenly closed. All that I could think about was how this girl, whom I was hoping to somehow impress with my janitorial job, was trying to do something great with her life. I somehow forgot the fact that I was also trying to do something great with my life, albeit in my own unusual way, and instead focused on the fact that Elizabeth was a woman who was above my level. I began to feel that it wouldn't be right to drag her down. I suddenly forgot that this girl didn't even know my name, nor had appeared on my last visit to be the slightest bit interested in me. I kept thinking that I had lost something great, something that, in actuality, I never had.

After drinking my hot chocolate I got up to go and tried to say coolly, "Bye Mr. Cheswick. And say hi to Issa and Elizabeth for me." Unfortunately, my voice cracked when I said the name of Elizabeth, revealing my affection, and it was at this time that the other customers in the café decided to look up and see who was talking. Starting to grow comfortable in my humiliation, I headed out the door.

Chapter 12

I'm ashamed to say that after my talk with Mr. Cheswick I once again fell into the grips of my own negativity. With one seemingly unimportant train of thoughts, my mind had caught hold of my heart again and was squeezing it into submission. It was like I had never left California, as all of the same insecurities surfaced to color and rule over my world. I felt less than those I loved and wondered at my own worth. Rampaging through my head were an endless stream of thoughts centering on the notion that I had made a terrible mistake by coming to Blue Bells, as there was nothing for me, or anyone to care about me here. I forgot about those friends I had and instead concentrated on the ones I wanted.

I tried hard to keep my miseries away from Mr. Landauer, as I felt they had no place in his house. And it truly was not hard, for upon seeing his innocent smile I couldn't help but smile in response. We passed the mornings playing cards and telling stories, although he never talked about his family, he usually told stories about his school days growing up. He talked about how he used to lead everyone in academics but when it came to sports or music, he was always the odd one out. This was the only time the smile would fade from his lips. When he would explain that as a child he was, 'a bit of a nerd,' to use his exact words, his eyes would wander and he would become very solemn. Though he loved to watch the school baseball games and go for the yearly music festivals in Cloverdale, he was a completely uncoordinated and physically awkward child. His mind though, was fast and energetic and he always tried to make up for his lack of physical skills by showing his mental toughness. This, unfortunately, developed into an aloofness that cost him many friendships and in the end left him a bit of a loner.

"While I was reading Plato and Kant," he explained, "those ninnies were chewing bubble gum and playing dice. I couldn't stand that they seemed to have more fun in their meaningless games than I had in my intellectual pursuits. I learned the ethics of Aristotle and tried to pass them on to my buddies but they all said that I was crazy and would call me "Professor" in jest. It's funny, because I knew that I could be a great professor, but hated to hear that name with all my heart. "Professor! Professor!" They used to call after me in that blasted high school! But it only drove me more into my books and my head and made me even more resolute in the rightness of the path that I was following. I didn't want to be like them until they finally shut me off completely. Then I was alone with my mind and my ethics and my knowledge. And I had nothing to hold onto. No friend. No family. All I had was my haggard memories that haunted my lonely nights."

On another day, he explained that his college years were a very earnest time for him. "I never thought that education's main focus should be to make money," he told resolutely. "I wanted truth for truth's sake. The more I studied, however, the more I found that real truth, unchangeable, unadulterated knowledge, was hard to come by. I knew that I couldn't attain material prosperity through my pursuits, but that was never my goal anyway. I wanted to be free from the delusions that bind us to what is not real."

Feeling that he was hitting on something close to my own problem I inquired of him, "What is it though, that is not real?"

"Even now it's hard to say. I'm getting old and I can't decide if nothing is real or if everything that I see is as real as it gets. I tend to think that reality is that which is unchangeable and look for that... but then again maybe my hypothesis is altogether wrong. How to really know? I'm old and maybe I'll find out the truth soon enough." This brought a mischievous smile to Mr. Landauer's face.

Other than this occasional walk down memory lane, Mr. Landauer was all smiles. I loved him but realized he must have some sort of haunted past that he tried hard to forget. I wondered at what my work companions had said about him, figuring that there must be some truth to it. Still, I never wanted to talk about it with them. I didn't in any way want to forsake the kindness that Mr. Landauer had shown to me by gossiping about him with the others. So I let it be enough to know that he was at least a good person now.

Chapter 13

Having the entertainment and distraction of Mr. Landauer's stories kept me on an even keel at home, but as soon as I left his house for work I became a sudden slave to my whimsical mind. My job was such that many hours I worked alone, as Ed and I divided most of our building up to save time. These long hours alone provided ample time for me to meditate on my worth, which at that time I felt was even less than the $6.60 per hour that I was being paid. It is funny to measure one's worth, of course, but this was a constant pastime of mine.

It seems my coworkers had also grown tired of my moodiness as one day while playing cards, Charley looked at me and said, "Would you just snap out of it, man. What do you think this life is for, just moping around all day? The only point is to find some happiness. Is it that hard? If you seek out sorrow you will surely find it, and if you tell yourself you're depressed then you won't be able to escape the feeling. At the same time, if you look in the mirror and give yourself a goofy smile, then you will have to laugh. Please, won't you give me that goofy smile?"

He was right. I did have to laugh at that! When I was in a bad mood being a janitor was the worst feeling in the world, and I would tell myself that I was at the bottom of the social ladder. But I have to admit that when I was in a good mood being a janitor was quite a nice job. Nobody was there to harass or bug me and I could work as fast or as slow as I pleased. Except for the pay, there were a lot of benefits to this kind of work.

That night, as I listened to the twelve rings of the bells, I thought of how many hours had passed since I had left California. I wondered how many more hours would pass before I became someone who I could be proud of. And I asked myself what it really was that I wanted out of my life. I could not even answer that question.

As we were walking towards our cars, I noticed a small fire burning in the distance to the west. It seemed to envelop Blue Bells' one tree in a dim halo. I suddenly remembered that I'd made a vow to visit this one spark of nature two months back and still hadn't been out to see it. The halo around the tree grew brighter for a moment and I asked Ed if he knew what that was.

"Oh, that's just the Tree Woman's fire."

"The Tree Woman?" I asked with a quizzical stare.

"Yeah, they keep that fire for her at night."

"A fire? For what?"

"Well, to keep her warm I guess."

I was completely confused. "Why do you want to keep the tree warm?" I asked, neglecting for now the obvious question of why the tree was a woman.

"Wait a second? Are you telling me you haven't heard about the Tree Woman? My God, she's like a local monument around here!" I just stared as he continued. "You haven't really had the 'Blue Bells' experience until you've met her!" Ed was starting to get excited while I was just getting more confused.

"What are you talking about? You mean there's someone who takes care of that tree? Like a crazy girl or something?"

"No, no, no! You've got it all wrong, my friend. Just shut up and listen for a second, because this is a really good story. This is like the story of Blue Bells. This is what makes us special as a town, you know. But we have to sit down for this so I can get fully into it."

It was getting late, and I was feeling extremely tired, but I figured from Ed's excitement that I would want to sit it out, so we huddled inside of Ed's car to escape the night's cold as he told me the story of the Tree Woman.

"Well, about forty-five years ago, as my dad tells it, this scrawny woman, with night-black skin and long matted hair, came stumbling, barely able to walk, into town. She looked as if she had been walking since the beginning of time..." Ed paused for a second. "Well, there are others who'll tell you she was really beautiful when she first came to town, and I suppose she would have been young, maybe in her twenties then, but anyway this is my father's version."

Ed sat up straight, eager to properly convey the mood of the story. "She was filthy and covered only in blankets. And as she walked it was like she was not at all aware of her surroundings, like she was in some kind of trance. She was wailing too. My God, I mean that she was so covered in tears that she couldn't have known where she was. She was simply moving and screaming. Some who remember tell that she was screaming about some dead children or something, but I think that no one really knows for sure. At any rate, this was the fifties and this town was as racist as any in those days, so the townspeople were not really concerned about what her problem was, they were just shocked at her trespass. It was a time when there were not many black folks around these parts, you know, and what few there were, were all grouped along the edge of town. They kept to themselves unless they had some work here and they always stayed quiet, trying basically to stay invisible. So this woman's presence in this white-only district was like a sudden shock to the residents. As she walked, more and more angry townsfolk were gathering around her, following her and shouting obscenities. I'm sad to say that my father was one of them, but he was just a kid, you know. Anyway, she somehow wandered near the school and that's when the people really started to freak out. Some were throwing stones at her and kicking her. But she didn't even seem to notice. She just kept getting up and moving on in her own world. And then, it was like everything stopped for a second, as this woman's eyes seemed to open up and she saw that tree over there in the distance. She was probably a good fifty yards from the tree but she saw it and a sudden peace fell over her. The townsfolk were confused, so they just waited to see what was going to happen. This woman just started walking towards the tree and eventually sat down right at the base of it. She again entered a trance-like state and simply stared at the sky. Well, the townsfolk wouldn't be having this black woman sitting fifty yards from their children, as it was somehow shameful to them, so they again started yelling all kinds of obscenities at her. But she didn't even notice; she just kept staring at the sky.

"Well, eventually this huge ogre of a man tore a branch off the tree and just slammed it across this woman's face. Blood starts pouring from her forehead into her eyes, and her eyes then refocused on the people. But she wasn't mad. She didn't cry. She simply looked at them in a kind of accepting way. And what could they do? One by one they left her, ashamed at themselves. My dad, though, says that some kind of presence came over them, because one second earlier they were ready to kill this woman and the next second all of their power was gone. All that they could do was simply walk away.

"That's amazing," I said in disbelief.

"No, I haven't got to the amazing part yet."

"What could be left?" I asked.

"After forty-five years," he continued, "the Tree Woman still sits there under that tree. She hasn't so much as moved to go the bathroom."

"You're kidding me?" I was completely shocked that such a thing was even possible.

"No lie."

"How does she survive?" I asked.

"Mostly now, people bring her food. But there were many years in the beginning that she never ate. Now people kind of go there out of ritual, seeking advice. She has a way of cutting through to the truth, and so when people have a problem they go and see her and offer her something to eat. But also, she's not so alone anymore, as there's that Elizabeth girl, who takes care of her."

"Elizabeth?" I asked.

"Yeah, this girl from John's Café. She goes out there every night to light the fire and clean her off. So at least she has some kind of regular attention, though that can hardly make up for the physical discomfort of it all. I can't even begin to comprehend the situation, really."

My focus was suddenly divided. I had just heard the most unbelievable and awe inspiring story that should have left me speechless, but the mention of Elizabeth's name brought a whole new perspective to things.

"Elizabeth, the girl from the Café?" I asked again

"Yeah, she's this girl from Costa Rica that works with Mr. Cheswick."

"Yeah, right. I only met her once, but I know who she is."

There was a moment's silence. Ed just looked at me peculiarly and then started laughing.

"I see, I see," he said with a laugh. "I just tell you the history of Blue Bell, and you couldn't care less! Yeah, I know this look! This is a new look for you to be sure, but there's no doubting the meaning of it. I cannot believe that you've fallen for Elizabeth."

"Hey now!" I answered, "I haven't fallen for anybody!" Unfortunately, fallen was indeed the correct word as I seemed to fall into the pit of hope and despair, mostly despair, every time I thought about her.

"She's a good friend of mine, you know. I could hook you guys up if you want. Though I have to warn you she's no ordinary girl. She's very strong willed and doesn't take any kind of crap from anybody. Still, she's a sweetheart all the same."

"No, no, no. It's nothing like that. I'm not looking to get hooked up and wouldn't want to impose on her with her studies and all."

"Her studies?" Ed laughed. "How do you even know about her studies? Oh man! How could you keep this from me for so long."

"You're dead wrong, Ed. Mr. Cheswick told me one day that she's in school, and that's the only reason why I know about it. Besides, I'm more interested in this Tree Woman right now." I tried hard to change the subject.

"Sure you are...Well you know you could visit both of them if you wanted. You could go tomorrow night while Elizabeth is there and that way you could say hi to her also, and she would take the attention away from you so that you needn't be scared about your first visit with the Tree Woman."

"What? I could go and visit them?" I was completely unsure about what Ed was getting me into and didn't want to make any rash decisions. "Is there reason to be scared?" I asked.

"Not if you don't mind someone reading your mind and knowing your every hope, desire and thought."

"Um..." I stammered.

"Yeah, you can take off early tomorrow. Usually Elizabeth goes out to see the Tree Woman at around eight o'clock, so you can get off by then and go and visit them." Ed seemed much more excited about this than me, which I figured was a bad sign. Especially if he was letting me get off work early to go and see them. I figured he was in it for the laughs, as real life provided the most entertainment in these parts.

"Um..." I continued.

"Great, it's settled then," Ed said with a slap on my shoulder to finalize the agreement.

Feeling both sick and excited by my coming adventure I made my way back to Mr. Landauer's house completely lost in thought. But I could hardly prepare myself, as the story of the Tree Woman was just too unbelievable to comprehend. And if Elizabeth wouldn't talk to me at the café, then what would she think of me showing up in the middle of a pasture in the dead of night? I knew that I wouldn't be able to sleep that night, so I didn't even bother going inside the house after arriving home. I instead paced up and down the walkway for the next four hours or so, as my mind spun around the stories of the day. Eventually, I passed out on the porch, not to awaken for some six hours when Mr. Landauer could no longer bear the sight of my spectacle.

Chapter 14

"What's wrong with you, Ballard?" Mr.
Landauer was frantically asking as I came to my
senses. I felt completely frozen after sleeping the
night away on the porch. For a moment I couldn't
remember why I was there, and then with a flash the
image of the strange Tree Woman and Elizabeth shot
back into the forefront of my mind. I had been so
possessed by the thought of them the previous night
that I was physically unable to sit down until I had
collapsed out of complete mental exhaustion.
Though I had never met this Tree Woman the
thought of her triggered something in me like a lost
memory that I was just trying to recall, but couldn't.

"I don't know," I told him. "I guess I was just
too tired to make it to my bed."

"Ballard?" repeated Mr. Landauer.

"No, I really had a long day yesterday."

"Ballard." Mr. Landauer was obviously aware
that I was keeping something from him. But I didn't
want to talk about the Tree Woman until I had seen
her for myself. I also didn't want him to think I was
crazy after spending the whole night outdoors, and
figured that talking about some probably mythical
woman, would only add to his worries.

"No, I just had a long day yesterday, and sat
on the porch to clear my thoughts, but I guess I was

so tired that I ended up falling asleep here." It was at least partially true.

"Well you're not kidding there!" he said almost angrily. "You were so fast asleep that I thought you were dead! You didn't answer when I called out, and when I started to push and shake you, you felt completely hard and frozen. Only after I started yelling at you in disbelief did you eventually come back to normal. It's too cold to be sleeping out here. At least take one of the sleeping bags if you feel in the mood again -- this old heart can't take the worry!"

I could only smile at Mr. Landauer's concern. And for a moment it put my restless mind at ease, picturing him jumping around my sleeping body. But the rest of the day would pass in full anticipation of what I would find when I ventured out to see Elizabeth and her Tree Woman.

The more I thought about it, the less I believed it. Since I couldn't fully wrap my mind around it I began to wonder if Ed had somehow discovered my affections for Elizabeth and had woven this elaborate story together to have a big laugh at my expense. I didn't want him to know that I doubted him though, so I kept all of my thoughts that night to myself.

It was no problem getting off work early. Lester couldn't care less when I clocked out so far as my work was finished, so I set out to complete my section in record time and was done by 8:00 p.m. Ed even helped with my side of the building, as he was even more eager than I was for me to meet the Tree Woman. But slowly what I was about to do began to settle in my mind and I realized that it was not going to be all fun and games. My excitement turned into nervousness, which turned into panic. It was pitch black and I didn't have any idea what I was going to say or do once I got out there. And as Ed saw me off, there was no convincing him to join me.

"Please man, it'll be so much better if you introduce me formally. It won't be like I'm butting in or something."

"But you are butting in," answered Ed.

"Wow, you are so kind," I shot back sarcastically. "You set this whole thing up for me, encouraged me to meet the 'monument of Blue Bell,' and you won't even accompany me there! Whatever happened to friendship, camaraderie, being there for one another? Where's the support?"

"Hey, if you really needed me, you know I'd be there."

"No man, I really need you!" We both laughed -- his joyous, mine nervous.

"But in all seriousness, I've been there enough and have no desire to return. There is no point in seeing the Tree Woman unless you want to see her. She will tell you as much herself. And this just isn't my day for that, okay? I can't wait to hear about your experience though. So... have fun," he said, gesturing me on my way.

"Sure, I'll have fun all right. Making a complete fool of myself."

"Don't worry, Ballard," Ed said with a smile. "Everyone already knows you're a fool!"

"Elizabeth doesn't know."

"Well, tonight she finds out!"

With that Ed sent me on my way, and I was left to wonder about what I was actually doing. If I wasn't scared before, the mystery combined with the darkness was now starting to weigh on my nerves. As I made my way towards the fire, I realized that I was indeed setting myself up. There was no way for me to come out of this looking good. Would I pretend to be just passing by? Should I try to be funny and just say, "Well I was in the neighborhood and thought I'd drop in?" It really didn't matter now because I was on my way. I just told myself that I was determined to find out what all this was about, though my determination was weakening with each passing step.

I walked through the field towards Blue Bells' only tree, but all that I could see was the fire in the distance. Every time I hit a rock or a ditch, I stumbled a bit and waited a second to be sure that they didn't hear me. I wondered if they would be less offended by me if I just ran up there loudly, making my presence clearly known. But my shyness kept me from any action that bold, and I instead went for the "Peeping Tom" method of introduction. As I got closer I saw that there were two figures both sitting on the ground. Soon I could identify Elizabeth's outline and it was clear that she was talking. But it looked as if she were talking to a smaller tree in front of the larger forty-five foot tree. What kind of game was this? Was my love crazy? But as I got closer I couldn't believe what I saw. The light shined clearly on the Tree Woman and I saw that she was indeed real.

Her skin appeared to be thick, like leather, and her hair was long and matted and seemed to be growing right into, or out of, the ground. There was no end to the bags under her eyes, while the rest of her face sagged so much I thought that it would just slip off. Her legs were stretched out straight in front of her and she was leaning against the tree, which I could now make out was a giant red oak. Her hands were folded in her lap but she would every so often lift her right hand to emphasize some point that she must have been making. I couldn't make out what she was saying but she talked in a very slow and deliberate way. Her voice was broken; it almost crackled like the fire. She had a number of blankets wrapped around her but I could tell from her arms and legs that she was extremely thin, seeming to only have a tough layer of skin hanging over her bones with absolutely no muscle or fat between them. She looked exactly like a tree that had somehow come alive.

It would seem from these characteristics that she should be ugly, but on the contrary she was the most beautiful woman I'd ever seen. If you can call her a woman even. She seemed beyond that distinction. There was something about her that was simply mesmerizing, unreal, or possibly more real, as

Mr. Landauer might say. I just stood shaking my head, forgetting that I was even there and feeling as though I were watching a movie.

As I was totally engrossed in my thoughts, it was a complete surprise when all of a sudden the Tree Woman's head turned towards me and I could clearly hear her say, "Why, Elizabeth, your admirer is here." Her deep grainy voice sent numbness through my whole body.

I waited for a second, hoping that I had not actually heard what I thought I'd heard. But when Elizabeth's head also turned in my direction there could be no doubting that I'd been discovered. For a moment I thought about turning around and running, as they probably hadn't seen me clearly, and I really didn't know Elizabeth well enough to care about the fact that I would never be able to show my face around her again. But I couldn't move, as my brain was on 'shut down' mode and seemed not to be in control of my actions.

"Come here," said the Tree Woman a little louder revealing an extremely horse and gravely voice. "No time for cowardice now, even if you're comfortable in it, for I don't have the time. Besides, you got this far so you might as well come the rest of the way."

Humiliated, I slowly walked into the light of the fire. From a distance of about ten feet I said, "I'm sorry. I shouldn't have come. You see I work over--"

"Come here," she interrupted. So I came closer.

"This is Issa's friend Ballard Davies," said Elizabeth.

Elizabeth's voice had a whole other kind of power. The nervous waves of a boy's confusion came over me, as I was completely shocked to hear that Elizabeth knew my name. And further, how she was associating me with Issa, whom I hadn't seen in months.

"Well, it took you long enough," said the Tree Woman.

"What?" I asked.

"I'm sure you meant to come sooner but you got so wrapped up in things. It must be hard for you, trying to do everything that you want to do. So many ideas, yet so little resolve and conviction. One act to your record you do have, but it will take so much more."

"But I..."

"I only have one question for you," she continued. "How does it feel?"

I had no idea what she was talking about. My brain was overloaded and my tongue heavy as I struggled to put some words together.

"How does it feel?" she repeated in a slow and failing voice. "How does it feel to have come all this way and to find out that you've gone nowhere? For it hurts even me to see it, so for you who are experiencing it, it must be excruciatingly painful. Still, it's necessary if you want to truly know, and even if you don't, I want you to know."

All I could do was stare. Though the rest of her body seemed dead, her eyes were amazingly alive; they seemed brighter than even the fire. Looking into those eyes of hers, I could hardly concentrate on what she was saying. But she went on, continuing to make the fool out of me.

"You tried in vain to leave it behind, that which is the source of all your problems, yet you hold on to it and let it be what defines you. You are such a funny boy, yet so typically inept in this way that I won't hold it against you." I was clueless as to what she was referring to, and the more I thought about it the more my head began to ache till it reached a point where I felt it would explode.

"Your mind is like a wild lion. If you don't tame it, how will you ever find peace?"

A few moments of silence passed, finally to be broken by the sound of the bells signaling that it was 9 o'clock. "Do you hear those bells?" she continued. "They are counting down the hours that you have to overcome yourself. No amount of hiding will allow you to escape this time. Time is your enemy, and if you don't use it, then it will absolutely use you."

I had no words to answer what I couldn't understand, so we sat in silence. Eventually, Elizabeth looked at me and said, "It's time for us to go." At first I didn't hear her, though I was aware that something had been said. Then she gently pushed my shoulder and repeated more forcefully, "Ballard, it's time for us to go."

"What about the fire?" I stammered.

"It will burn itself out by morning."

We got up and walked away. The Tree Woman seemed to be sleeping, although she was still sitting up against the tree, and her eyes were wide open.

As we neared the school I realized that I still hadn't said anything meaningful to Elizabeth. I wondered if she were angry with me for disturbing their peace. She seemed in no mood to talk but I couldn't help myself.

"The Tree Woman is truly remarkable," I said.

"You mean Grandma Daisy."

"What's that?"

"The 'Tree Woman' is not a nice name at all. Only the gossips use it. Those who love her, call her Grandma Daisy, because there are always daisies growing around her. You'll see them if you ever come back in the daytime."

"I'm sorry to have interrupted you both."

"It's not a problem. You're welcome to come anytime. She's there for all of us."

With that we made it back to our cars. I had the rest of the night off and so made my way home, more confused than ever. When I arrived I immediately went to Mr. Landauer's room where I found him reading one of his philosophical texts. I still couldn't believe what I'd seen and asked him if he knew Grandma Daisy.

"Oh. So that's what you've been up to." Mr. Landauer had obviously still been concerned about finding me asleep outside in the morning. "I met her a number of times years ago, but haven't seen her in at least twenty years. I always found her very inspirational but at the same time very intimidating. How can you relate to someone who understands you better than you understand yourself? And how do you think I felt in realizing that I didn't understand myself at all? Certainly not the ideal for an old man! And I was old even then! But the way that she can seemingly have nothing, but be even more content than someone who has everything, can't help but make you feel as if you're taking life for granted, you know."

"It's true," I said. "Seeing her in that most wretched condition, I still couldn't feel as if she were lacking anything. It was like she was filled up by some unearthly spirit or power. She was completely contented in her poverty and it gave her some kind of peace."

"Ah, Ballard, you too might become a philosopher yet!"

"Well, I don't know about philosophy but I know I can't wrap my brain around what happened tonight."

"She opens our minds to the possibilities."

"And there's this girl, Elizabeth who takes care of her..."

"Oh yes. Elizabeth of the Café. I've heard about her."

"Have you?" I inquired.

"Nothing much. Just that she attends to the Tree Woman. That she came from some foreign land, and that she had a hard life."

"A hard life?" I asked.

"Well I don't know the specifics but when you find out you can tell me, okay?"

I went to bed that night and dreamed constantly about the Tree Woman and about Elizabeth. I saw myself at that campfire under the stars and I remembered clearly those brilliant eyes of Grandma Daisy smiling at me. When I awoke the next morning I was a little scared at how she seemed to have taken over my thoughts. I resolved not to go and see her again until I'd talked to Elizabeth separately about her. But in fighting to free my mind of her image it seemed that her image only became stronger and stronger within me.

Chapter 15

The next day at work dragged on longer than normal. I couldn't leave the previous night's magic behind and felt oddly sad that it was something I wouldn't be able to repeat. I, of course, was free to go visit Grandma Daisy anytime, but felt like it wouldn't be right. One night's interruption would be tolerable, but if I kept going back, I was sure they would soon weary of me. And I was anyhow committed to not going until I understood more about whom it was that I was visiting.

All day I simply went through the motions of my daily routine while reenacting the conversations with the Tree Woman over and over in my head. The other janitors didn't bother me, thinking that I was just in another one of my moods, but Ed knew the reason for my distraction. I, however, couldn't bring myself to talk about it with him. I couldn't understand what I saw and at the same time didn't want to make light of it. Ed, knowing the situation, tried to hold his tongue. He seemed more concerned than anything, as if he were responsible for doing something that might have hurt me. I could see him thinking of things to say to me, but, like myself, he just kept his mouth shut. Eventually, though, I saw Ed's face light up as if he had discovered what would rectify the situation.

That night at cards Ed finally broke his silence and said to me, "You know what you need, Ballard? You need a night at Saul's. Anyone who sees Saul's situation can't help but feel better about his own!" All of the janitors laughed at this.

"It's sad but true," said Charley. "Saul's predicament seems to create happiness for everyone else. Not that he's living for the good of humanity, but it does humanity some good to take a break and watch."

"Who's Saul?" I asked.

"Forget it, Ed. Don't take him there. Saul's nothing but a Scrooge," said David. "People love him cause he has money, but I can see through all that. I never found anything good in him."

"Come on, David," said Charley, "there's some good in everybody. It might be harder to see with some, but there's something there." All of the janitors, even David, continued to laugh, but I had never even heard Saul's name before tonight, so was clueless as to what all the commotion was about.

"Don't listen to David," said Lester. "He's just sore cause he couldn't scam a job off him."

"As if anyone ever listens to me," said David with his usual gruffness. "And actually that's a good question. Why is it that none of you ever seem to care about what I say?"

"'Cause you're rude... mean... emotional... yet never rational!" said Lester.

"The man has a point," added Charley, with the enthusiastic agreement of Steven.

"Listen," continued Ed. "There's a dinner party at Saul's house Saturday. None of these other jokers are allowed to go as they've all, even Steven sadly enough, acted rather rudely on previous occasions. But Saul still has faith that I might have one or two good friends somewhere and always says I should bring them by if they're decent."

"Hey, we're decent!" cried David. "Just because I laughed when I saw them. You should have warned me!"

The others broke into another round of laughter and I, wanting in on the joke, asked, "Warned him about what?"

"Well, you see," started Ed.

"Their situation is a little unique," added Lester.

"A little ungodly!" said David.

Even Steven was getting in on the fun. Lifting his arms, as if to show his muscles, he jumped around like Superman, and then came crashing down to the ground and started shaking his head in mimicked remorse.

"Exactly," said Charley. "So sure of himself, yet so pathetic. That is the unfortunate nature of Saul."

"He's not pathetic," pleaded Ed, "just eccentric."

"Eccentric is a nice way to put it," added David.

"You see," continued Ed. "It started back... I guess it started when Saul's father, before I was born, moved to Texas and made a lot of money in the oil industry. He was married for a brief time there and had a son, Saul. When Saul was about ten, his mother passed away from some sort of cancer."

"No, it was tuberculosis," piped in Charley.

"And it wasn't oil, it was textiles," said David.

"Textiles?" asked Lester.

"Whatever, whatever... So then Saul and his father moved back here. They bought the biggest house in town. Saul became a classmate of mine and we hit it off real fast."

"That's not the way I heard it," said Lester. "I heard that you dragged around him till he couldn't help but notice you. That he only felt sorry for you because he thought you didn't have any other friends."

"All lies, complete lies... anyway, so... I had plenty of friends man."

"That's not what my daughter says," stated Lester, to another round of laughter.

"Um...where was I?" asked Ed.

"You and Saul were best of friends," said Charley.

"Oh yeah. So, Saul is very popular and has these three girlfriends. All three are very beautiful, and all three are completely different from each other."

"Is one of them Lester's daughter?" I asked, trying to keep up with the story.

"Hello? Lester's daughter has nothing to do with this story," cried Ed in anguish.

"You see, my daughter and Ed used to go out but it turns out that Ed was too eccentric for her."

"Okay," continued Ed. "Thank you for the added comments but, as I was saying, Lester's daughter is a non-issue here and forever more in my life, as I have no residual feelings for her. But at the same time as our most uninspired dating, Saul was going out with three other girls. Got it?"

"Got it," I confirmed.

"So, eventually he decides to marry one of them and has a kid with her. But after about five years his father dies in the middle of some family business scandals and Saul goes through some minor depression. In the midst of this he rekindles his love for one of the other original three girlfriends. He divorces his first wife, but it becomes financially more feasible for her to stay living in their enormous house, than to be kicked out of it and get half of his money. So, anyways, after some time, he marries this second girl."

"So he moves into a new house?" I question.

"No," said David, "He's living in the same house with his second wife and his ex!"

"What?" I asked. "That must be unbearable for him."

"Wait, it's not over yet," said Ed with increased enthusiasm and growing animation. "So, then his second wife gets fed up with him and decides that she doesn't like the way he lets his first wife run the house and eventually she divorces him. But once again he finds it financially better for her to stay at home, and she is more than happy to lose herself in the back half of the house."

"Oh, that's so sad," I said.

"Wait a second," cried Ed.

"Saul is very educated, but when it comes to these sorts of things..." Charley was not able to finish his sentence, only shake his head.

"Don't tell me!" I said.

"Exactly," said Ed. "Saul meets up with his third old girlfriend, and he just knows that she must have been the right one from the start."

"Oh, no!" I cried

"Oh, yes!" cried Lester.

"For the love of God!" called David.

"So then," Ed went on, "Saul ends up marrying this third girl. But she had no idea of the situation at home. She becomes instantly disgusted with Saul but somehow becomes good friends with the other two wives. Seeing that their situation was quite good, she decides to divorce Saul and live as friends with them all."

"So Saul lives with his three ex-wives?" I ask, for confirmation.

"It's a regular house of sin," said David.

"Oh, I'm pretty sure there's no sinning going on over there," said Charley, sending Steven to the floor shaking with laughter.

"Actually," said Ed, "the man has renounced love altogether. He has taken to reading philosophy and writing books."

"That's what he says now, but just wait for another pretty girl to come walking by and it will be the same old story," said Charley.

"No, Charley," said Ed, "Saul's really changed now. You wouldn't even recognize him."

"What do you mean? I saw him last week at the supermarket."

"Charley!"

"Just kidding, Ed. I know what you mean."

"This sounds like an interesting family," I said. "But I'm not sure I'd want to be in the middle of any dinner party with them."

"Oh no, you'll love them. Believe me, they're so much fun and I think you really need to have some fun for a change!"

"Yeah, maybe that is what I need."

"It is! So meet me here Saturday evening at seven. OK?"

"OK," I agreed.

My mood had completely lifted. The Tree Woman's tug over my mind became less as I anticipated what the dinner party at Saul's would entail.

Chapter 16

Saturday morning brought much expectation on my part. I was ready for a fun and entertaining time. Noticing my mood as we drank our morning coffee -- of which I was now the maker as my coffee was much smoother than his -- Mr. Landauer asked me about why I was so happy.

"Tonight I am going for a dinner party at these interesting people's house. It is the family of Saul and his three ex-wives."

"You're going to Saul's home?" asked Mr. Landauer. "When I left town he was still married to his first wife, though I'd met the others in other circumstances." Mr. Landauer stared up at the ceiling, lost in thought.

Eventually, I asked him, "So, you know this family?"

"I used to know them well, but now they're just a part of my past."

"Oh, well did you want to come for the dinner? I could ask Ed. I'm sure it would be alright."

"No, I'm sure it wouldn't be alright..." He seemed almost angry for a second, before he continued; "You might hear some weird things about me when you're there. Just know that I have a history with them, and let them say what they want."

"Oh... If you don't want me to go then I won't go." I was worried about the look on my old friend's face. I didn't want to be the cause of any disrespect to him.

"No. Actually, I really want you to go. They are a nice family, after you get to know them. Anyway, you really need to get out more. Someone of your youth should not be cooped up all day with old fogies."

"Hey, you're not an old fogey!"

"I'm nearly eighty. I don't know what else you'd call me."

"But you hardly look fifty," I argued. With a laugh, Mr. Landauer finished his coffee and went out for a walk.

These remarks left me even more curious about the family. I didn't want to be in the middle of any bad blood between Mr. Landauer and them, so I figured that I would just leave out the fact that I was staying at his house. Besides this, I still couldn't believe that anyone would hold a nervous breakdown against an old man.

Seven o'clock couldn't arrive fast enough for me. I had practically enacted the whole dinner party in my head five or six times without even knowing how any of them looked. But when the time finally arrived I was nearly jumpy as I met up with Ed in front of the school.

"Calm down, man. I don't want them to feel like they're on display or anything. Just act cool, okay?" Ed looked a little worried.

"No problem. No problem. I'm just excited to be doing something. You know, it's been a few months since I've done anything besides work, sleep and cards. I'm just a little excited, that's all!" I couldn't wipe the stupid grin off my face no matter how hard I tried. Ed shook his head and told me to follow his car to the house.

We left the school and headed north towards the residential district. This was the first time I'd driven in this area. For the first ten blocks, the houses were quite small, but as we made our way north the houses became bigger and bigger. Eventually, we closed in on the end of the town where the houses were mansions. In front of one of the biggest of these, we stopped. This, of course, did nothing to calm my nerves and my grin only seemed to be getting worse.

As we started walking towards the house, my ever-active imagination kicked in and I realized that if the people matched the house, it meant that I would be very underdressed in my button down shirt and slacks, with no tie, and no jacket. My only consolation was that Ed was dressed even worse in his dark T-shirt and jeans. I mentioned my apprehension to him but he told that these were just normal people with an abundance of money and a weird living arrangement.

We didn't bother to knock; Ed just opened the door and we walked in unannounced. The house opened up into a large entrance room with marbled floor and a high ceiling. There were marbled stairways leading upstairs on both sides of the room. We walked straight through, turning into an opening on the left that led into a living room the size of three of Mr. Landauer's houses. There were three couches semi-circled towards a giant fireplace. In the far corner sat a grand piano and an acoustic guitar was propped up next to it. In the center of the room stood a young man around my age. He was dressed in blue slacks and a tan shirt with a blue tie and blue jacket. He had closely cropped brown hair and a two-day-old beard. He stood up straight with an air of aloofness, but that all broke down into a huge smile when he saw us.

"Hi, guys. You must be Ballard, right? I'm Saul."

"It's nice to meet you. Thank you so much for letting me come over. It's an honor." Ed looked as if he were going to be sick at my giddiness.

"Oh, well you haven't been here too long yet. I'm sure by the end of the night you'll see that the honor was all ours, as we need the entertainment here. Not that you are entertaining, but we don't get enough visitors. My exes will be down in a minute. I assume Ed has told you our whole history? I don't want the shock of his previous friend's feelings to be an issue again."

"Yes, he's told me your whole story," I said, again slightly too excitedly for Ed.

"Oh, well here they come," said Saul.

In walked three beautiful and playful women. He introduced them in the order he'd married them. They were all of the same age but looked distinctly different from each other. His first wife, Emma, was tall, and had long blond hair, and big blue eyes. She was dressed in a loose-fitting dark blue dress that extended just past her knees. She stood with a dignified air that was nullified slightly by her huge smile. His second wife, Rachel, had short brown hair; just long enough to tie back in a ponytail. She wore blue jeans, a gray t-shirt and was barefoot, with red nail polish on her toes. His third wife, Amber, had long, and thick curly black hair that she kept tied back in a big ponytail. Her skin was night black and almost shining. She also wore blue jeans, and a black t-shirt but wore large gold looped earrings that added an elegant touch to an otherwise playful appearance. All three of them, as well as Saul, looked quite familiar to me, as if I'd met them all before, but couldn't quite place where. At any rate, the exes were quite a threesome. They laughed and talked loudly with no need of hearing our responses. They instantly put me at ease, seeing that I wouldn't have to work at all at the conversation.

My first surprise came in the form of loud footsteps running down the stairs. When she came into the living room, I couldn't hold back my shock. I simply called out her name. "Issa!"

"Ballard! Hey how have you been?" she said, running over and giving me a hug.

"How do you know my daughter?" asked Saul.

"She's *your* daughter?" I said, amazed. "Wow, that's great! You know, she's the one who brought me to this town."

"No!"

"Yes!"

"No! What I mean is..." Saul was taking his time as he had something to say. "So you are the one who slept for weeks at the side of the road in your car?

"Yes!"

"And you are the one who is now living in my grandfather's house?"

"What?"

"Yeah," piped Issa. "Every week when I take the groceries to his house, your car is there."

"Mr. Landauer's your grandfather?" I asked, completely shocked.

"Well, he's my poor dead father's father. He's the reason this town's fallen into economic distress. He's the bane and humiliation of my life. He's a good for nothing old man and I can't believe that you've come into my house to remind me of him."

"No. He's such a sweet and lonely man who's only wanting for company," I pleaded.

"You have no idea about him!" said Saul.

I looked around the room and all were shocked except Issa and Ed.

"You knew about this, Ed?" Saul asked.

"Yeah! Come on, I thought this would be fun. It's like a family reunion... Almost! Come on, Saul, you must admit it's a little funny. I've been planning this for a month, so be happy at least for show!"

Saul only shook his head in disbelief. His face had turned completely red and he seemed to be talking to himself in his head, wondering which parts he should share with us.

"But Saul," I said, "you should know that he has told me about his breakdown and about running through the streets naked, and that he is so embarrassed that he had to leave the company of this city."

"I'm sure that he told you about *those* things. But did he also tell you that he used to be mayor of this town? Did he tell you about how he wanted to change our local government into a monarchy, making himself the king and that he actually tried to create legislation that would only allow the smartest people to rule? Did he tell you that he squandered the retirement plans of the whole town in the stock market and that he was the first mayor of Blue Bell ever to be impeached? Did he tell you that I had to change my last name to do business in the surrounding areas, as his name is forever damned by all who repeat it? Did he tell you that his wife was so embarrassed that she left him to run off with some trucker just passing through? Can you even imagine a sixty year old woman running off with a trucker?"

"Then grandma is not dead?" asked Issa.

"Oh... oops," said Emma. "Sorry, Issa, that was a secret." Her mother said this in a not very consoling way, trying both not to laugh and to be sweet.

Looking around the room, I realized where I had seen all of these people before. After making the connection I couldn't hold it in. "I know where I've seen you all. Did you know that Mr. Landauer has painted all of you on the walls of his home? When I first visited him, he told me that these were all of his dead relatives that he painted so as not to forget their faces. Oh wow. I'm sorry if I have caused any friction here."

"No, don't worry about it," said Amber. "This is the most fun we've had in three months. Anyway, it's not your fault."

"Yeah, it's Ed's fault," said Rachel.

"Thanks," was Ed's smiling reply.

My next surprise then came with the entrance of the next and final guests. Suddenly, from around the corner came Mr. Cheswick and Elizabeth. My heart suddenly raced to an even faster pace, as the night became alive with possibilities.

"Ah, everyone is here," said Saul. "Do you all know each other? Yes? Ok, fine. Let's eat." Saul seemed resigned to another disastrous evening at the hands of another of Ed's friends.

Chapter 17

The dining room centered around a large, marbled rectangular table where we all took our seats in elaborate hand-carved, oak chairs, under the lights of a giant chandelier. Saul sat at the head of the table with Mr. Cheswick opposite him. To the left of Saul sat his three wives and Issa. To his right were Ed, myself, and Elizabeth.

Issa said grace and we all took what we wanted, passing the rest around. There was cauliflower soup, salad, mashed potatoes, and some spicy mixed vegetables. Saul explained that Emma, Amber and Issa were all vegetarians so the rest of them would suffer accordingly.

Ed and Saul immediately began talking about some local politics and building rights. Emma, Issa and Rachel chatted about a tennis match they'd watched, and Amber and Mr. Cheswick spoke of history and the plight of a nearby Native American reservation. That left Elizabeth and me to try and make some kind of intelligent conversation. She handled the intelligent part and I just tried to put some words together.

"You seem exceedingly happy about something."

"So, I hear you're in school," I stupidly stammered as my head was spinning from the sound of her voice.

"You're excited because I'm in school? Well, you must be a very considerate person then." She was toying with me, and I didn't know how to respond. My mouth became dry and I mentioned the only other thing that I could remember about her.

"So... You're from Costa Rica, right?"

"Yes, though I've been here for the past four years." Her face softened as if she'd decided she didn't mind talking to me.

"Oh, four years? How old are you?"

"I'm twenty-five. And you?"

"Twenty-seven, a college drop out and a janitor!" I figured I should lay it all on the line.

"Well, you seem quite proud of yourself."

"So, how did you make it to this town?" I asked, again quite oblivious to the flow of the conversation. I was only concerned with trying to keep the conversation going. But then the subject turned serious and I regained control of my senses.

"That's a long story and I'm not sure it's interesting enough to tell."

"No. Please tell me. I don't know anything about anybody in this town. I just want to get to know people. For real, you know?" It was only partially a lie as Ed had told me gossip about half the residents of Blue Bell, but about Elizabeth I knew nothing and wanted to know everything.

She then began to tell me the story of how her family pushed her into marriage at the age of seventeen. After three torturous years with a husband that beat and lied to her, she told him that she wanted a divorce. He was drunk at the time and flew into a rage. He ran out of the house taking their two-year-old son with them. As he got into the car, they played tug of war with the baby. Elizabeth was forced to let go so as not to harm her son. The husband sped off, eventually running head on into a big rig heading in the opposite direction, killing himself, her son and the driver of the truck who was himself the father of three. She spent the next six months in a daze, mostly crying. At this point the family's priest, who was an American missionary, suggested that a change of scenery might do her good. He told her that his brother had an extra shack where she could live and a coffeehouse where she could work, if she wanted to move there. He told her that his brother had lost his wife and had dedicated his life to helping kids, and that he had two adopted kids from Puerto Rico who were now grown up. She decided to take him up on this offer and still works for this brother, Mr. Cheswick. She told me that she is going to school on borrowed money from Mr. Cheswick and that she plans to become a child therapist, or social worker for the school after getting her psychology degree.

Moved by her plight, I fell even more under her sway.

As the night went on, the conversations became more and more spirited. The subject of religion somehow came up between Amber and Emma, who were arguing over its purpose. Amber insisted that religion was something created to institutionalize morality, while Emma countered that it was really meant to be a beginning that should lead to a life of self-reflection.

"Self-reflection?" asked Saul in a voice loud enough to capture the attention of the table. "We all know where you get *those* ideas from and I'm sure you really don't want to get started with that. But I just have to add one thing. You have to admit that without science you won't have the freedom or time to even think about such things."

"What do you mean?" asked Emma. "Nowadays people know that science and religion are simply two paths that are in search of the same goal - - understanding. Why should you have such a problem with it?"

"Exactly," added Amber. "It's all about understanding. One seeks to understand the world and the other to understand ourselves. But more than that, one seeks to control the world and the other its people."

"No," said Emma. "Spirituality is not seeking to understand people in hopes of controlling them, but rather to understand ourselves, in order to become truly free."

"You put too much stock in this understanding one's selves," retorted Saul. "What nonsense. Science is the height and breadth of knowledge. All else is just hope and desire, based on emotion, speculation and delusion!"

"Yeah, sure," started Issa with some sarcasm. "You can praise science over art and meditation, but science always starts out as creative ideas in the mind of an artist, or creative thinker of some kind."

"You see, Ballard," said Saul dryly, "Issa is an artist and is under the impression that all geniuses are artists of some kind, because they see the world on a different level."

"Maybe not a physical artist," continued Issa, "but at least a mental one."

"You tell 'em," said Rachel.

"And when those mental ideas turn out to be sparks of brilliance," said Issa while shaking her head with increasing passion, "only then are the sciences built up. They all start with these original ideas."

"And what we have here," added Saul, "is the usual romantic idealism of women!"

"But doesn't she have a point?" asked Mr. Cheswick. "It took Socrates and Plato to light the fire in Aristotle, the father of science. While he was a genius in his own right, he needed that initial spark of the masters."

"John," began Saul. "Please don't talk to me about history. What's history but propaganda, anyway? The winners have one story, and the losers its opposite. Math and science at least can be tested and has the integrity of its methodology."

And for a brief moment all were silent. I thought maybe someone would try and change the subject.

"Yeah, but can I say something further," continued Issa. And I must say I was on the edge of my seat for whatever this little girl had left to say.

"Science is so mechanical. It's always taking things apart but it takes real creative thinkers, the people with real wisdom, to put all of those pieces back together. Now these people might call themselves scientists, for credibility's sake or whatever, but really they're like the old-time philosophers. They are the real artists."

"That's it, Issa!" yelled Saul, in fun. "No more home schooling for you!"

"Hey, I didn't teach her those things," said Emma.

"Oh yes," continued Saul. "She is just a product of her mother's propaganda."

"No," said Amber. "She's more a product of Daisy's!"

I could see Elizabeth suddenly tense up at the mention of Grandma Daisy. Until now she was enjoying the lively conversation and I sensed she didn't want to have to take part in it by having to come to Daisy's defense.

"Grandma Daisy doesn't spew propaganda," started Elizabeth. "She is only there to help and inspire people."

"It's true," said Emma. "Daisy's main wish is to make each of us better people. She only wants us to live up to our potential."

"Hum," said Rachel. "Same old story, different day."

"Is there any better story?" asked Issa.

"My God, no more!" started Saul. "I don't want to hear anymore about this Daisy and her moralistic philosophies. In this world, the fittest, the smartest, and those with the most cunning, rule. That is the way it's always been. These ideas of hers are just a method that weak people use to supplant the strong. But anyone with enough sense will just push her out of the way."

"Dad!" cried Issa. "How can you talk about Grandma Daisy that way?"

"She is not my Grandma, for one!" fought Saul. "And she is not yours, either. What she's doing is filling my daughter's head with ideas that will leave her ill equipped for dealing with the real world!"

"It is the world that is not equipped to deal with or understand her," answered Elizabeth.

"The world has no need for Daisy," said Saul, trying to be funny but not bringing a smile to anyone's face.

"You're wrong!" cried Issa. "The world ought to fall at the feet of Daisy, and indeed all of nature has come to serve her except pigheaded old men who are too stubborn, proud, and self-righteous to clearly see the gift that her life is to us!"

"Okay, enough" said Amber. "I started this by bringing it up... Let's just drop it now."

"All I'm saying," continued Saul, "is that you can have all the idealism you want, but if it doesn't conform with reality then there is not much use in it except hopeless aspiration -- the pastime of dreamers."

"And all *I'm* saying," said Issa, "is I would rather be a wise servant than an ignorant king. You can keep your strength and your comforts for I will any day trade it in for a little knowledge."

"And that is why it will always be people like you who are wiping the counters where people like me eat!"

There was a sudden hush as Saul's last comments stung most of the guests, as they thought mostly of Elizabeth.

"Don't everyone become reverent for my sake!" said Elizabeth. "For I too would take the wise servant option over the ignorant king." The gathering all laughed awkwardly and wisely moved on to less sensitive subjects.

Chapter 18

After dinner we all went into the living room to relax, a little stuffed and worn out.

"Why don't you sing something, Rachel," asked Amber.

"No, I'm too full right now."

"Come on. You know you live for these moments," Amber smiled.

"Like you wouldn't believe," answered Ed.

Taking their places on the floor, Emma and Saul took each other in their arms and stood prepared to dance. They both looked expectantly at Rachel.

"Okay, fine. Ed, come on." Rachel said as she moved to the piano bench.

Ed took the guitar and began to play a slow bluesy, jazz tune and Rachel, who had an incredible, booming voice, that filled the room, seemed to make up lines on the spot and sing over him. Singing a sad lonely song, the two of them looked as if this was what they were meant to do. Suddenly, Ed and Rachel became a moment to remember. The entire atmosphere was filled was a beautiful pain, and melancholy that sprang from their song.

Saul and Emma held each other and swayed to the music. Looking at them you would forgot that they were no longer married. The rest of us just sat with our eyes closed and reveled in the moment.

Later they switched to some fast Latin style folk songs that Ed had picked up somewhere and they all implored Elizabeth to dance. Elizabeth, to my surprise and horror, insisted that I dance with her. I pleaded my case, being completely unable to keep up, but couldn't withstand the force of her gesture and happily showed off my two left feet. She was dancing fast along with the beat, but I was forced to cut the speed in half and danced a slow wiggle from side to side. I can honestly say that I'd never had so much fun in my life.

The rest of the night passed in peaceful conversation and I fell in love with both families. Upon returning home, I found Mr. Landauer waiting for me.

"So, how was it?" he asked with a tentative stare.

"It was wonderful."

"But, did they tell you about me?"

"Yeah, they did."

"So?"

"So?

"So, what happened?"

"What happened?"

"What happened at Saul's?"

"I found the one!"

"What?"

"I've found the girl I've been waiting my whole life for."

"What? You fell in love with one of his exes?"

"No. With Elizabeth."

"Elizabeth?"
"Elizabeth."

Chapter 19

"So," said David, rubbing his hands together in anticipation of what I might say. "We won't be starting cards tonight, fellas, until Ballard here confesses all that he saw this weekend at Saul's. No gloss this evening. We want the meat and the dirt of it, complete with facial expressions, she said, he said, and how many times did you in fact have to say, 'I'm sorry I didn't mean it like that.'" Steven showed his agreement by gesturing for me to sit down while he took over the coffee making duties for the night. Ed slid back in his chair and put his feet up on the table with hands behind his head and a big grin on his face.

"What can I say?" I asked. "It was great."

"Yeah, Ballard fit right in over there," said Ed. "Not like you guys."

"Thanks, man," said David sarcastically.

"So you liked Saul, then?" asked Lester.

"Well," Ed interjected, "I was smart enough to invite Elizabeth, so Ballard here really didn't even know that Saul was there." Everyone laughed at this, but I was still feeling high from the night before and didn't take offense to it.

"So you're sweet on Elizabeth?" asked David, nodding his head as if answering his own question.

"Hey, I'm not sweet on anybody," I lied.

"It's all right," said Charley. "This small town life is unbearable for young people unless they're sweet on someone."

"Hey, it's not bad for me here," I said sincerely. "At least I have you guys."

"That's true," said Ed. "There's nothing like the company of a bunch of old men who think they know everything, to set the heart aflame."

"Yeah," answered David. "It's almost as nice as being around a couple of young boys who think they have life down to a science!" Again everyone laughed.

"Is life not a science?" asked Ed. "Who in this room is not predictable? Whose story couldn't I tell?"

"But seriously," asked Charley, "what did you think of Saul? He can sometimes be a little intimidating at first."

I thought for a moment, not wanting to answer dishonestly, and at the same time not wanting to offend Ed.

"Well," I started. "He has good choice in wives."

"'Tis true, they're all great," said Ed.

"I mean," I struggled to continue, "I really like Saul as a person, he was really relaxed with us so I can't say that he was intimidating; rather I would have to say he has some weird ideas. But if his family can put up with them then I don't know why I should be bothered. I suppose he seemed a little confrontational, but I think that might just have been in the heat of a family battle and I don't want to hold it against him. He may just have been playing around, but since I don't know him well, it was hard to tell how serious he was at times."

"Oh, he was serious all of the time," Ed said.

"What kind of ideas?" asked Charley.

"Well," I really didn't know where to begin.

"You know, Charley," said Ed. "The same old stuff about idealism teaching ineptitude when it comes to dealing with the world." Ed tried his best to say this as dryly as possible as he rolled his eyes. I only then understood that it was a long played out argument from Saul.

"Oh, *those* ideas," said Charley with a smile. "Don't worry about that, Ballard. You really can't take anything Saul says seriously with all of his lofty ideas because he's got them all from books and hardly understands them himself."

"Really?" I asked. "Because he seemed pretty sure of himself, and argued all of his points quite clearly."

"To be certain," continued Charley. "He understands what he's saying but he doesn't at all understand that to which he is applying his words, namely the world. Saul has a pride that comes with scholastic knowledge. A pride that is hard for anyone to protect themselves from. Knowledge can either help or hurt us, and with him it has only served to puff up his already oversized ego. For all of Saul's 'relate to the realities of real people' talk, he has no 'real' experience working with 'real' working people."

"Yeah, that must be true," I said.

"Unless a rich man comes out of his castle," continued Charley, "and lives among the common folk, he can never really understand them. But one day too, his world will come crashing down around him, as it happens to all of us. Maybe then, he will be able to better connect with the 'realism' he so covets."

"But hasn't his world already come crashing down so many times before?" I asked. "Three wives, two dead parents, a runaway grandmother, and an exiled grandfather all seem pretty tragic."

"No, Charley is right," said Ed. "At this point he still has everything he wants. He still has his three girl friends and he simply feeds off of his relationship with Mr. Landauer. But eventually we all must suffer, and his time will come for that."

"'Tis true, young ones," added David. "'Tis so very true."

Chapter 20

Since the dinner party at Saul's, I'd lost all control over my mind. I thought only of Elizabeth. I went to the coffeehouse every day - even when I knew she wasn't there, in a vain attempt to hide my partiality. I thought only of the possibilities of the life that we could have together. I imagined our big house, our two children, our pleasant evenings, our long walks, and our dedication to each other. I even imagined bringing the rest of her family over from Costa Rica and that we would have a full and happy household.

I, of course, never bothered to mention any of my fantasies to her. I merely assumed she was thinking along the same lines as me. And if she weren't, I figured, with enough time, she would come to love me also. I knew that I didn't have anything I could offer to such a woman as her, but still, I felt there was a special magic between us, and that any obstacles would be overcome by the power of this bond.

In order to try and recreate the merriment of Saul's party, I suggested one night to Ed that we all get together and play music in the park near the school.

"No man, I don't want to get chased from that park."

"Are you kidding? You guys are good. Anyway, it would be a lot of fun and I think that people would really like and appreciate it. We could even leave the guitar case open like beggars, and I bet you we could make some money."

"Sure, Ballard," said Ed. "But not enough money to make it worth it. Anyway, I need my weekends to rest up."

"To rest up from what?" I asked.

"From all of this hard work we're doing!"

"We haven't worked a day since I started here."

"Hey now!" said Ed, taking a joking offense. "We may not do a good job, but we definitely work!"

"Okay, I'll give you that. But come on, Ed. It'll be fun."

"Well, who all were you thinking of inviting" Ed asked slyly.

"Everyone from the party could come."

"Oh, you mean everyone as in the 'it doesn't matter if anyone else comes as long as Elizabeth is there' everyone. Is that the everyone to whom you were referring?"

"Ed... it would be lots of fun and we never do anything fun around here. Rachel's voice is so good and I could clap and Elizabeth could dance and it would be really fun."

"Not that you're not a great clapper and all, but, didn't we just do that last week?" he asked with a smile.

"You can't tell me that you didn't like it."

"No I loved it, but part of the joy comes because it doesn't happen everyday. I don't want to wear out my welcome with Saul and all. Besides, if you want to go out with Elizabeth you needn't bring me along. I'm sure that she would be agreeable to just the two of you."

"Come on Ed, it's really not about that at all."

"I'm sure it's not," Ed said as insincerely as he could.

"Don't you want to make music, man? I know that's what you love. I love it too, and just want to be a part of it."

"Yeah, but I don't want to make music boring."

"You can't make music boring! Ed, I don't know what you're arguing for anyway. You're just simply being difficult for the sake of being difficult."

"Yeah, so?"

"So stop it! Come on! I want to have fun! I want to forget that this is just a stupid, small town. No one cares about anything here. Can't you guys just break out of your stupid routines for even one day?"

"Didn't you just tell Charley earlier that you love it here?"

"Ed!"

"Okay. Okay. I'll ask Rachel about it tomorrow."

"Great."

"Actually, we can call her right now."

"Now you're talking!"

We called Rachel from one of the teacher's offices and she immediately agreed. She said she was always ready to play music at any time of the day or night. She promised to convey our invitation to the rest of the family and whoever was interested would come to the park Saturday morning.

We then called Elizabeth, or I should say Ed then called her. She was shocked to get our call although she knew that Ed had her phone number. She took a little more prodding from us, but on the agreement that we wouldn't make her dance, and also that Issa would be there, she eventually consented and we made plans for the upcoming weekend.

"Okay," Ed said to me. "You owe me one!"

"Hey, I'm doing this for you man!" I lied. "I want to showcase your talents!" We laughed and got on with our work.

Chapter 21

"Oh. No Saul, or Emma?" I asked, seeing the group gathered Saturday morning at the park. "Who's going to dance, then? Even Amber didn't come?"

"No," Rachel began, "they were busy with some work and all. They like to dance but you have to drag them to go anywhere."

The park was basically an open field, save for a single jungle gym, where families were having picnics and kids were running freely.

"Well," said Elizabeth, "we should probably find somewhere quiet."

"Hey, but Ballard there is intent on making some money!" cried Ed.

"No," I said. "We can sit anywhere. I don't care."

We eventually agreed on a secluded area so as not to disturb those who didn't care to hear us.

Ed had brought some bongo drums for me to play, along with a tambourine for Elizabeth. Neither of us were much good at these instruments, but it didn't much matter because Ed and Rachel were so talented that it made up for what we lacked. We were just happy to feel involved and played with complete abandon, like fools, on instruments we didn't know.

As Rachel became more energetic and emotional in her singing, Issa began to dance, and after a few minutes a large crowd began to gather around us. It was like a real concert. People would clap and sing along to songs they knew and just dance and jump to the others. Kids would call out the names of songs they wanted to hear and if they were lucky, Rachel would sing them. If Rachel didn't know the song, then she and Ed would just pretend to ponder the requests until eventually a kid would call out the name of a song she knew. Everyone felt as if they were getting a real treat and contributed almost fifty dollars to our empty guitar case.

Afterwards, we decided to spend our earnings on ice cream. We sat there for hours laughing, telling stories and generally enjoying each other. Elizabeth's face was so bright and vibrant the whole day, as if she'd forgotten her previous troubles and was sincerely happy for our company. I couldn't have asked for anything more.

Not wanting the night to end, we just kept getting refills of coffee, but around nine in the evening we noticed Amber and Emma walking outside. We banged excitedly on the window to get their attention. They looked very anxious as they noticed our faces through the glass. Upon entering the parlor Emma called out, "Rachel, where have you been? We've been looking everywhere for you!"

"We've been here. What's the big deal, I told you we were going to the park."

"It's not a big deal," said Amber, "only, you know how Saul worries. He's had us out looking for you for the past two hours."

"Well, I don't like all that! And I don't have time for it either! I'm my own woman and I'll stay out as much as I want!"

"Hey now," started Amber, "don't get mad at us. We were just trying to calm him down. But now that we know you're safe, we'll give him an update and he can go to bed. Anyway, he'll feel sad he missed out since Ed and Ballard are here. He really had fun with you guys at the party."

"Oh!" I said, surprised. "He could have come. I told Rachel... Oh..." I felt stupid again, having put my foot in my mouth. Still, I was sad that Saul hadn't received the invitation. I didn't want to increase any friction between Rachel and him though, so figured I'd better just keep my mouth shut.

Reluctantly, we decided that we'd call it a night, and so saying our good-byes, we went our separate ways.

Chapter 22

One Sunday afternoon, about a month removed from my first conversation with the Tree Woman, Elizabeth told me she and Issa were going for a visit and asked me if I wanted to come. Elizabeth, of course, saw Daisy everyday, but as Issa was coming, they had decided to make an afternoon picnic of it. Although a little apprehensive at the thought of seeing the Tree Woman in the daytime, I didn't want to pass up the opportunity to be around Elizabeth so I readily consented. We all met in front of the school, everyone sporting unusually big smiles; they were ready for a fun afternoon, while I was merely trying to conceal my tension.

Issa seemed especially excited, almost giddy. I wondered what sort of relationship Issa had with Grandma Daisy. I knew she had defended her vehemently against her father, the night of the dinner party, but I didn't know how much of that was to prove her point and how much was coming from a sincere love for Daisy. Whatever Issa said though, was always said with great conviction, so I suspected only the sincerest of intentions from her.

"How long have you been coming to see Daisy?" I asked her.

"Since I was in the womb, actually. My mom used to come here everyday while she was pregnant with me. She said that Daisy used to sing to me while my mom would rest her head on Daisy's lap. I guess she would just make up these songs about the nature of the world and how everyone is always looking to cheat his neighbor to get ahead of him in life. You know, real baby talk."

"What kind of tunes were they?" I inquired.

"Oh, mostly kind of blues chants, or hymns and things. She doesn't sing to me anymore though, so I'm just going on what my mom used to say. But my mom said they were so mesmerizing. That they cut deep into the nature of the world and would always cause her to cry, but would cause me to calm down inside, as I guess I used to move around a lot."

"So Daisy is really like family for you then?"

"Oh yeah. Grandma Daisy is even the one that gave me the name Issa. My father was, of course, completely against that, as he never cared anything for her. Not that he doesn't like her, but he thinks she's a bit crazy and says that she has no business showing the way to the rest of us. He just can't see what we see in her. I think he's a little jealous and wishes that we'd ask advice from him for a change. But when you have someone like Daisy who holds the world in her hands, why should you waste time with someone who is merely guessing at it?"

"Sounds reasonable enough," I said.

"Indeed."

"Okay, you guys, let's get going," said Elizabeth. "I told her that we'd be coming today so she'll be expecting us."

"You told her that *I* was coming too?" I asked, as Elizabeth had only asked me hours ago.

"Yeah. I knew you'd say yes!" said Elizabeth, putting her palms up as if to say, "Of course, you'd do anything I asked." And, of course, I probably would.

Elizabeth gave me a bucket of water and a basket full of wood to carry and we headed out to meet Daisy. As we walked towards the red oak, my stomach tightened. I didn't know what to expect from this visit. I was glad that Issa was with us and hoped that she would take some of the attention away from me. I wanted very much to see Daisy in the light, as she was such an intriguing character, but I didn't want to be subject to any questioning that would make me feel stupid, as I gave myself enough of those opportunities on my own. Even more than this, I was afraid that she would read my mind and reveal some embarrassing thought to Elizabeth.

As we were walking, I saw for myself, for the first time, the reason for Daisy's name. Although there were no other flowers in this field, the area surrounding Grandma Daisy was completely covered with daisies, stretching out twenty feet from her in all directions. It looked like a halo surrounding her figure, enhancing the supernatural feeling that engulfed her, and leaving me completely dumbstruck.

When we neared, Issa answered my wish as she made a jubilant scene, running up to Daisy and giving her a kiss on the cheek.

"Issa! It's so good to see you again. It's been some months. I was wondering if you were keeping away from me."

"No way. Mom is really strict with my studies lately. That's all."

"Why the sudden change?" asked Daisy.

"You know, Dad. He's been worried about something or other and it's been making Mom even more stressed. I think he's been having some troubles with his job or something, because he's been real moody lately."

"I told Emma, the day she told she's marrying that Saul, that he would slowly drag her down with him. I know she still tells herself that she loves him, but she's just scared to face the world alone. She's forgotten the woman she once was."

"Mom still talks about you all the time, though."

"Oh?" asked Daisy suspiciously.

"She still defends you and praises you."

"I don't want her defense. Only her embrace. I love her like my own daughter. Like I love you."

"I know," said Issa cuddling up to her.

"Try and get her out here. Emma was always so playful and emotional. That was always fun for me, but it's been almost two years now.

"She's still playful sometimes," said Issa. "But she's more tired these days."

"Tired how?"

"Just tired in general."

It was strange for me to hear this conversation, as I never would have thought of Saul and Emma's situation in this light. I wondered if seeing Daisy was their biggest point of contention.

Daisy was very animated on this day. She talked with Issa in the most natural of ways and I was shocked that they were not having more of a serious exchange. My previous encounter with Daisy led me to believe that she was all business, but these two were talking like old friends.

Daisy could move around a lot more than I had previously thought her capable of. Although her legs didn't move, and were stretched forward, still in the exact same position as before, both of her arms were moving up and down. She would even lunge forward and grab Issa from time to time. Until now I had imagined that her back had actually grown into the tree.

I was quite happy just being a witness to these events, but eventually Daisy looked over at me and my heart raced.

"Ballard. It didn't take you too long to come back. I suppose that for the love of another we tend to become more courageous. At any rate, I'm happy to see you."

"It's nice to see you again also," I said, trying to smile. Trying to look casual. Trying to breathe.

"And how's the whirlwind upstairs?"

"Whirlwind?"

"You know. What we talked of before. How is the mess in your head? Is it any better?"

"Yes, it's much better, thank you."

"It's better because your situation is better. But when someone is mean to you, it will again start to turn. The one thing we need to control in this world is that one thing that we never seek to master."

While we talked, Elizabeth was busily preparing our lunch. She had brought a basket which was full of fruits that she was cutting into small pieces. She then divided the fruits among four plates and poured four cups of milk from a flask that she had. As we ate, Daisy again turned to me and began talking.

"The fruit is so soft because I'm such an old lady. I can't eat anything that I can't squish!" Everybody laughed.

"You know, Ballard," she continued, "when my husband and my children died, I didn't think I could go on living. They died driving to a show where I was to perform. I was an actress in those days. It was just a small town play but they were so proud of me." Daisy looked straight into my eyes as she talked. "I couldn't stand the pain of losing them, so I just began to wander. I didn't eat, I didn't sleep, I just walked and cried and screamed and prayed.

"Somehow, I made it to this town. When I saw this tree out here, it was just a small young tree then, I was somehow inspired. It was all alone out here in the middle of nowhere. But somehow it was growing. It started as nothing. Just a seed - probably planted by some kid. And from that seed grew a young tree. And from those twigs would eventually grow this grand oak that would one day give shade and sustenance to others. I somehow realized that I was like this tree. I was alone, in the middle of nowhere and I had to survive on my own. It was not yet my time to die. I decided that if this spot were good enough for this tree, then it would be good enough for me. And under its shade, and with the comfort of God, I have also survived. I'm able to give comfort to others and I live on the love that they share with me.

"I've learned," she continued, staring almost through me, "that it's very hard to understand life without suffering. Suffering is a great teacher that most people run away from instead of trying to learn its lessons. Without suffering we would never pray, or think, or try. So don't run from your problems. Embrace them. Analyze them. Use them to grow stronger and wiser. And then you can truly reach your potential and develop into a good person."

When Daisy spoke, I couldn't help but stare at her mouth. She said each word as if it were coming from deep inside of her. Her lips were old and cracked, but the words were full of meaning and her low, husky voice screamed of a reality that was pure.

After we finished lunch, Elizabeth took out a small book of poetry and began to read. The book was filled with the songs of slaves who had escaped to freedom. Issa laid her head on Elizabeth's lap while Daisy closed her eyes and listened. We passed a good two hours like this, and I felt as if I were completely transported to another world. Never in my life had I listened to poetry before. And I never could have imagined that I'd spend two hours doing it. But today was a special day and I was completely open to whatever was happening.

The sun began to set and Elizabeth said that she had better give Daisy her bath before it got too cold. She took a sponge and the bucket of water over to Daisy and began to wash her off. She wiped down her face, her arms and her legs. Then she tried uselessly to scrub her hair, which was thick with dirt. She took some wood from the basket I'd carried and put it in a small pit that was surrounded with stones and rested a few feet from Daisy. Here she started a fire and gave the excess twigs to Daisy to toss in as the night passed.

We then said our goodbyes and headed back towards the school. Not wanting the night to be over quite yet, I struggled to think of something to say. "Where did you get that wood from?" I eventually asked.

"There's a huge forest in Cloverdale, the town where I attend college," Elizabeth said. "The trees there are so old and beautiful. I go there as often as I can just to relax and clear my head. I wish I could take Daisy there, as I know she would love it, but she's too old for that now and really has no interest in those kind of things anymore. You should come out there some time, though. It really gives you a new perspective on things to see life that has been around hundreds of years before you were ever thought of."

"I want to see Cloverdale also," said Issa.

"Then we'll have to make an outing of it sometime," replied Elizabeth. "You guys will love it."

Chapter 23

Amber showed up at work. She seemed to know exactly where to find us. Looking at Ed mischievously as if they'd already rehearsed this conversation she said, "You know there's that play in Merced running right now."

"Yeah, heard about it," he responded mechanically.

"Saul was mentioning that the two of you should come."

"Well... it's up to Ballard."

"Up to me?" I asked. "What do I have to do with it?"

"Come on, Ballard," said Amber, "Saul really wants to have some guy friends come along. He's sick of going everywhere with just the ladies."

"Oh, so *you* don't want us then?" I joked.

"We'll be there, don't worry," said Ed. "Ballard's got nothing else to do."

"Hey now!"

We drove that night in two cars to a neighboring city, Merced, and met Saul's clan in front of the theater. They were certainly a sight. Saul with his three ex-wives, seemingly in perfect harmony. They were all laughing and playing together like kids. Ed, Issa and I pulled up the rear as we entered the hall, admiring the sight of the four of them.

"Saul looks like a King!" I joked.

"Yeah, sure," said Issa, "a king with fool's gold!"

Somehow when we took our seats, I ended up between Amber and Emma. I don't know why I was between them, as they were only interested in talking to each other, and did so nearly throughout the entire performance. Though they spoke in whispers, everything they said was funny. They constantly picked at the actors, and I had a hard time not laughing out loud.

"Does he really seem like a cop to you?" Emma would ask, literally pointing at the actor in question.

"No, he's way too skinny for a cop!" responded Amber. "But look at those eyes. So beautiful!"

"And his butt is nice also!" added Emma.

Later, switching to the heroine, "My God, is that the best they could do? She's so homely looking."

"Come on, Amber," said Emma sympathetically. "She's really trying."

"I guess. But she dances all right."

"Yeah, she dances fine but what is that girl in the back row doing."

"Does that count as dancing?"

"Why put her in a dance sequence?"

"Maybe she can't act."

"But she's kinda cute though."

"Yeah, kinda."

On and on it went for the whole show. Fortunately our group was so big that our whispers didn't seem to bother those in the next row. Not that they couldn't hear us, but maybe we just scared them.

As we left to go our separate ways, Saul pulled me aside. "Hey, you should really come around more often. You seem to put everyone in a lighter mood."

"I don't think your family needs any help getting into a lighter mood."

"No really," continued Saul. "You can come by anytime. You're part of the family now. You don't have to wait for events like these to visit."

"Thanks." It was just a small comment, but it meant a lot. I was finally part of a family that wanted me.

Chapter 24

Owing to a bet Rachel had lost to Ed, Rachel was forced to feed him one home-cooked meal. Rachel was not at all used to cooking, as she went straight from her mother's hands to Saul's maid's graces. This being the case, she recruited me to help. Not being a cook myself, yet not wanting to miss out on the fun, I agreed to cut the veggies.

"Uh... So what should we make?" She asked as I entered her kitchen.

"Hey, you haven't figured that out yet?"

"No. So?" She was not at all concerned. I guessed that Ed was probably not expecting much, considering the situation.

"Well, you said you'd cut the veggies," she reminded.

"Yeah?"

"So, which veggies do you want to cut?"

I smiled, realizing why she'd wanted me to come five hours early. We were only cooking for five. Emma and Amber would be coming with Ed later. Issa had gone with Saul to Cloverdale to complete some business transactions.

"We're cooking for Ed, so what does he like?" I asked, while looking through the contents of their freezer.

"Oh, he loves to go to Cloverdale for fast food!"

"Great! There just happens to be frozen French fries right here."

"There are?" asked Rachel. "We never eat those here."

"French fries!" cried Emma walking into the room.

"Hey, you're not supposed to be here yet!" shouted Rachel.

"Well, Ed said he was too busy to entertain me so we agreed to all meet here."

"Oh."

"What are you doing with my french fries?" asked Amber, entering the room.

"Oh, so these are yours are they?" asked Rachel.

"Well, I get hungry in the night... We have veggie burgers too!" she said with a grin.

"Sorry?" asked Rachel.

"Sorry for what?" I blurted.

"Sorry, I didn't understand what you said..." giving a dramatic pause for emphasis, "*veggie* burgers?"

"Don't start, Rachel. They're really good."

"Um. No thanks."

"Hey, but I heard Ed say he liked them once," added Emma.

"He did?" Rachel didn't seem to believe it, but the thought of how easy they might be to make was holding some weight over her decision. "How long do they take?"

"Three minutes each," said Amber with a knowing shake of her head.

With the menu settled, we used the spare time to decorate the dining room. We took the table out of the room and put five cushions in a circle on the floor, loading up the burgers on a plate in the middle. In front of each cushion we set a plate with a knife, a spoon, and two forks each, all beautifully unnecessary for our hand to face meal.

At last we heard Ed's knock at the door. "I'll get it," I said on my way to the door.

"Good evening, sir," I said with a bow.

"Ballard! Hey, I didn't know you were going to be here."

"This way, sir." I led him to our luxurious dining quarters.

"Wow! Rachel? You did all this?" We were all happy to see Ed's apparent shock.

"Well, I had a little help from my friends."

"Okay. Okay." said Emma. "Let's have a toast."

"A toast?" asked Amber.

"An orange juice toast," said Emma.

"Oh. Fits the health theme," said Rachel.

"Um, french fries aren't healthy," inserted Ed.

"Those are veggie burgers," whispered Rachel

"What?"

"Get over it," Emma said to Rachel.

"We baked the fries though, we didn't fry them," I pointed out to Ed.

"What? You didn't fry the fries?"

"No, but they're good, so don't worry," I said.

"So, the orange juice toast," reminded Amber.

"Oh yes," continued Emma, raising her glass. "I just wanted to say that it is times like these that really help to remind us of the beauty this world actually has to offer."

"*Actually*?" asked Amber.

"Wow, that was beautiful," I said.

"But why did she say *actually*?" asked Rachel.

"She didn't mean it like that," defended Ed. "It was just free style."

"Thank you, Ed," nodded Emma.

"Though, maybe it was a subconscious thing," continued Ed.

"Shut up," said Emma.

Chapter 25

Feeling emboldened one morning while eating my breakfast with the old men in the Café, I decided I would have to make a strong and affirmative move if I ever wanted my relationship with Elizabeth to go anywhere. When Elizabeth walked over to my table to say Hi, I took the opportunity.

"Elizabeth."

"Um. Yeah, that's me."

She smiled. And for a moment that was enough. But then I remembered my conviction. "You're always the one serving me breakfast."

"Yeah, that's the way it works here."

"Well, how about if I take you out to breakfast for a change?"

"All of my days off, I'm at school." She didn't say no! I didn't expect her to say no, but I was still excited.

"That's okay. I'll drive out to Cloverdale and meet you. We can go out to lunch on your break."

She looked slightly amused by my persistence before answering, "Okay."

"Okay!" I said excitedly. "That means yes!"

"Correct. But it has to be between one and two thirty."

"No problem."

"Wednesday, then?"

"I'll be there."

That left me five days to figure it out. I made my way to Cloverdale each morning and visited every restaurant, coffee house and food shop I could find. I taste tested all of them until at last I found the perfect one.

The day arrived and found me circling the university's administration building for the better part of the morning. This is where we agreed to meet, but not having anything else to do I hung out there until our scheduled time. When she finally arrived, I couldn't control my excitement, or my smile. She got in the car, examining my face with amusement but saying nothing.

We drove east through the town for about fifteen minutes before Elizabeth finally said, "I've never actually been to this part of town before. How did you know about it?" Ah, sweet contentment.

"Hey, I have my connections too!"

"Sure."

Finally, we pulled up to a small little restaurant called El Sabor de Costa Rica. Elizabeth stared with shock at the sign.

"Ohh. That means the flavor of Costa Rica," she said dropping her head slightly and squinting as if her eyes were failing her and she needed a better look.

"I know what it means." I was so proud.

Inside was even more impressive. Though it was a restaurant, the walls were like a museum, covered with photos and paintings of famous historical figures and monuments. Excitedly,

Elizabeth took me to each picture and explained it. I'd never seen her in quite this mood before. She completely lost her normal reserve and was almost giddy.

There were only two other guests in the restaurant and the manager didn't seem to mind our milling about. Eventually, we sat down and our waitress came over. Elizabeth asked her where she was from and the love fest began. They talked a good fifteen minutes before we ordered.

"Wow, Ballard. This is the best surprise you could've given me."

I just smiled.

"I never would have known this place existed. I'd forgotten how much I love to just talk in Spanish, you know?"

"Yeah, I thought that you're always working and you needed a break. This is the closest thing to a vacation I could think of."

Reaching out over the table and grasping my hands she said, "Ballard this is so great. This is perfect. You really did it for me."

Now, I know she didn't mean it in the way that I took it, but I couldn't help it. She had touched my hand and now I would completely lose any sense of reality in our relationship. My mind became a veritable altar for the love of this girl. This scene would be played over and over again in the film room of my mind. And I was freeing myself to drown in the ocean of her love.

Chapter 26

The next day, I saw Elizabeth talking to Ruben Bennet and Phiser Mitchell. Normally, seeing these two would make me uneasy, but on that day, I had a surprising confidence and didn't think twice about having to defend my lack of a living philosophy. My head was still in the clouds and I had no problem walking up to them with an enormous grin on my face.

"Wow! How's everyone doing today?" I said rather loudly, moving my hands around in the fashion of Mr. Cheswick. I then started clapping and shaking my head as if I was cheering them on to a response.

"Well, well," said Phiser. "You are certainly looking up today."

"Huh," said Ruben, looking at me suspiciously. "No 'Mr. Bennet, Sir?' No cowering of the shoulders? Elizabeth, what's happened here?"

"What's that look, Mr. Bennet?" I laughed. "Come on now. You can't bring me down today." I was smiling irrepressibly.

"Elizabeth," said Ruben with a disapproving frown on his face.

"Don't worry, Mr. Bennet," said Elizabeth. "He's just been working too hard lately. He's a little worn out and getting punchy."

Looking over at me with a fake seriousness she mumbled, "Ballard..." and shushed me away.

Chapter 27

Early one morning, I got an excited phone call from Elizabeth. It seemed that Daisy had called for Emma, and after having heard from Issa that her mother was staying away due to Saul, Daisy demanded an immediate visit from Saul. Elizabeth, thinking that I wouldn't want to miss this historic visit of such divergent minds, invited me along. Needless to say I rushed off to Daisy's tree.

As I was walking from the parking lot, I could see that Issa and Elizabeth were both already seated next to Daisy. All of a sudden Issa stood up and anxiously looked in my direction. I knew her worried face wasn't for me, and turning around I saw the family. Like a gang they made their way nervously towards Daisy. None could look up. Instead they stared at the ground, trying to feel their way along.

Suddenly Emma broke away from the group and ran towards Daisy, patting me on the shoulder as she passed. Dropping to her knees, she kissed Daisy's hands again and again, saying, "I'm sorry, I'm sorry," through her tears.

"Time hasn't changed anything," said Daisy. "You look to be doing good enough. Just barely, but sometimes good enough is all we can hope for."

"Everyone is getting along so well at home these days," Emma said.

"Oh, and you don't want to destroy that?"

"It's not that, but the calm is a nice change."

"But at what price?" asked Daisy.

"No price."

"Then?" she further questioned.

"Then what?" asked Emma.

"Then why has it been so long? I've waited so long to see you."

As Emma paused, the others arrived as if to answer the question for her. They all sat in a semi-circle around Daisy, and the previously mournful faces instantly turned playful, like kids. All that is, except for Saul. Saul stood proud with his arms crossed and his teeth clenched. Not being able to match Daisy's eyes, he simply looked at her feet.

Daisy greeted everyone individually, like family that she hadn't seen for awhile. Then finally she slowly turned her head up towards Saul. And for a couple minutes, they just looked at each other. Daisy at Saul's eyes, and Saul at Daisy's feet.

"Well, old man," started Daisy, "you've finally made it."

"What?" asked Saul. "*You're* calling *me* old?"

"To me you seem very old."

"I don't know what you're expecting from me, but don't think I'm going to play these silly games."

"To me," continued Daisy, "you seem like a senile old man who can't even remember the purpose of his life."

Saul's expression turned to one of shock.

"I thought you're supposed to be full of love and grace, old lady." From all that he'd heard of

Daisy he'd never imagined her to be this confrontational. He knew instantly that he was unprepared.

"Let me remind you," continued Daisy. "You think that you'll lose Emma to me. But don't worry, because not only did you never have Emma, but also you have plenty of other more pressing problems to worry about.

"Daisy, please," pleaded Emma. "Saul is not used to all this."

"I can speak for myself," said Saul.

"Speak for yourself?" asked Daisy. "You hardly know yourself, let alone can you speak for it."

"Yeah, yeah," said Saul. "I know, old lady. You know me better than I know myself, right? Whatever. It's easy to read people. They are like machines. Everyone basically reacts the same. It's no great talent you have. You're just herding the sheep."

"You think that I prey on the weak," continued Daisy.

Saul shook his head a little.

"But actually," she explained, "I prey on the darkness in order that these children can see. Whereas you cling to the darkness, Saul, merely for its comfort. There is no real security there. The worst part is that you have studied all of the spiritual philosophies, but like an academic. After understanding them, you close the book and go to sleep. There's no real understanding there, because there's no real experience in it."

"And I need *you* to understand *my* experience?" grimaced Saul. "What nonsense."

"Yes, I know Saul," began Daisy. "You are such a great man. So many men are waiting to fall at your feet in order to do business with you. But why is your home empty almost every night? Because none of these men, who know you're great at business, care at all for your personality.

"What use is your great intellect if it leaves you cold and heartless? As compassionate as a brick wall. It is true that even a brick wall will provide shade for some plants and weeds, but that is merely by accident. Its main function is just to divide the properties. You are like this brick wall, creating divisions everywhere. And the funny thing is that you think this is what makes you great. A real man won't divide, but unite. In the presence of such a man, all will feel peace - not fear. So many so-called 'great' men have used fear to conquer, but they have all been risen up against. Only love can truly conquer a man's heart. Until you can truly offer love to the world, you will even be afraid of yourself. Because you will never be able to measure up. Your own hatred will suck you up like a black hole. Don't think that I'm cursing you. I only want you to be filled with this love."

There was a moment's silence but Daisy seemed suddenly finished with Saul. Turning to Rachel, Daisy asked, "Issa tells me that you sing beautifully."

"What can I sing for you?" she asked.

"Sing your new song," said Emma.

Rachel then started to sing a sad lonely song about going through your whole life without ever truly feeling loved before eventually breaking down and crying herself.

As she cried, Saul turned away and slowly walked back to his car. I had a feeling that he was crying as well, but couldn't stand for his family to see it.

Chapter 28

Because of the strength and scope of my ego, I don't like to talk about my purely illogical and rather stupid actions without prefacing that sometimes through the most foolhardy of expeditions the most profound lessons are learned. It so happened that on this particular night I was so blinded by the greatness of my imagined perfection that I attained to new heights of stupidity. But I was also blessed with one of the great lessons of my life, and a conversation that became a desired, though not always practiced, blueprint for all my future actions.

Although I knew very little about Elizabeth, I had somehow figured that her every second was filled with anticipation for our next meeting. I decided to bring profound joy to her heart by showing up at her house in the middle of the night. A midnight surprise would be romantic and show my undying love and dedication of which she, I knew upon seeing, would be forced to finally melt into my arms and curse all the days we'd been apart.

It might be noted here that Elizabeth had never given me her address. I obtained this information from someone who'd made me swear to secrecy that she was my informant. I'd also made her swear never to tell I'd asked for such information. This informant was, of course, Issa, who showed me herself to the alley behind Mr. Cheswick's house.

From here she pointed to the little cottage in his yard where Elizabeth stayed.

Upon arriving at the cottage, Issa left to sneak back into her own home, and I stood alone at the front door of the woman I knew was waiting for me. I knocked on the door, excited beyond belief, but there was no answer. I knocked again and then heard a little movement inside.

"Hello?" came her voice from within. "Mr. Cheswick? What's wrong?"

"No it's me!" I answered with full confidence.

"Me, who?" came her response.

Me who? What was this? How could she forget the sound of my voice so soon? Didn't she have it repeating over and over again in her head as I had hers?

"It's Ballard. Ballard Davies!" My confidence was slowly starting to wane and in that brief second before she opened the door I realized the absurdity of my showing up in the dead of night at a house I'd never been to. The only thing that kept me from running away was the fact that I'd already revealed my name to her.

"Ballard?" she questioned as she opened the door. "What are you doing here? Is something the matter? What's happened?"

"Nothing's happened," I said, slightly concerned for the safety of my own, suddenly fragile, ego.

"Then?"

"Then what?" I asked.

"Then what are you doing here?" she repeated. "Or more importantly, how did you know where to find me and what business could you possibly have that is so urgent you needed to come here in the middle of the night to convey it?"

"Oh... I'm sorry. I'd heard you lived in a cottage out here and I couldn't sleep so I was just wandering around town and thought there could be a chance you were also having the same problem. I became convinced of this fact actually, and so decided to just check and see."

As I was telling her this, Elizabeth just kept shaking her head as if to say, *I see, I see, you really are a fool!* But instead of this she said, "No, actually I was sleeping quite well."

"Oh, well, that's good."

"It is quite a long walk from Mr. Landauer's house to here. You must've really been restless."

"Um..." I couldn't answer.

And that was it. I waited for her to invite me in, but she just waited for me to leave. I supposed that the correct answer would have been for me to just say goodnight and humbly admit my defeat, but my romantic ideas would not let me give up so easily.

"Did you want to come in?" she finally asked me.

"Uh... Okay... well..."

She shrugged her shoulders and fully opened her door. I walked into her two-room cottage, the first room having a kitchen, a table with two chairs and a mat for sleeping, and the second I assumed was her bathroom. I immediately noticed the cleanliness of it all. Elizabeth sat down at the table and motioned for me to also take a seat.

"Hum. Did Ed put you up to this?" she asked.

"No! Not at all."

"Because I would expect this kind of thing from him. He is always pulling pranks, so I wouldn't hold it against you if that was the case."

"Will you hold it against me if that's not the case?" I asked.

"Well... That remains to be seen."

I looked around the room and saw that everything seemed to have a place and an order. There was nothing untidy in this room. Every utensil on her counter was pointed in the exact same direction, every book was lined up perfectly according to height on her shelf, and she had even folded her sleeping blanket back up and had placed it neatly on the end of her mat before answering the door.

"You have a very nice place here."

"Thank you." She didn't really seem to care, but at least she was polite. I searched my mind for something to say, but ended up just spitting out more of the same.

"It is very tidy and organized."

"Well, sure. The state of your room shows the state of your mind. How can you have a clear thinking and clear seeing mind, which is hard to control, if you don't even keep these outside things orderly, which are so easy to control." She seemed a bit irritated, but I told myself it was due to the late hour and not to my company.

"Oh. Well, I guess that's a nice way of thinking about it."

"It's not just a way of thinking, it's practical advice." She said this with a smile and a laugh.

"Oh, I'm pretty clear thinking," I said defensively.

"You clearly can think, but you're not clear thinking. And you certainly aren't practical."

"Come on," I said playfully. "I'm pretty practical."

"Really?" she asked.

"Yeah. I think so."

"Do you know me so well as to be at liberty to come to my room in the middle of the night?"

"Um..."

"Did you forget," she continued, "that I'm a single girl and this wouldn't look so good to pretty much anyone who might have noticed you sneaking around here?"

"I wasn't really sneaking around," I begged.

"This is the first time you were here, it must have taken you some time to find it."

"Not really."

"Not really?" she asked

"In the middle of the night you knew exactly where to turn in off the alley?"

I thought it best at this point not to answer as I didn't want to give Issa up, and Elizabeth seemed to be right on pace to find her out.

"You have to remember," she continued, "that this is a small town, where no one has small mouths, and I'm pretty sure that your visit will be the talk of the gossips tomorrow if anyone did happen to notice you."

"But I'm not having any malicious intentions. I think that people here know me well enough by now to know that I have good character."

"A good character?" she asked with surprise. "How can you learn the character of a man in a few months? Our character is not so easily seen, you know. You can't just commit some good deed, or uphold to some higher moral philosophy on some occasion and be considered someone who is truly of good character. Rather, it must be there in every small action of your life. Perfection in character, Ballard, is perfection in every movement, thought and word. I don't know you well enough to know the true bent of your character, but I can see that your actions and thought processes are a little bit sloppy."

She said this sternly, so there would be no mistaking her seriousness. She then stood up and looked out the window. I didn't know if I was supposed to follow her or stay put or ask some intelligent question, or better yet make some intelligent response. So I just sat there waiting for her to continue with her undoing of my self-image.

"You know, when I came to this country I didn't know a lot about the ways people here interact, but I knew at least respect for my elders, and to look at the big picture before I start messing around with the small. Those two things were enough to get me by until I learned the finer points of small town American life. I know you have respect for everyone, Ballard, but you seem to have a great capacity for missing out on the overall place of things."

"What are you referring to, exactly?" I asked, as I was starting to lose her.

"Why are you even here, Ballard?"

"Well... I just wanted to see you."

"No, not in this house but in this town. What do you think was the reason you came to *this* exact town?"

"Well, it was just an accident."

"Was it?" Elizabeth's eyebrows rose as she turned and looked at me still sitting at the table.

"Yes. I just drove until I couldn't stay awake anymore. I was in a daze when I parked near this town."

"But what made you decide you couldn't stay awake anymore? Are you sure it was just an accident? Have you learned anything in this town you wouldn't have been able to learn anywhere else?"

"I don't know."

"Well, why don't you think about that?"

"Okay... I will."

Elizabeth had gradually moved towards the door and she now opened it, saying, "Well, it's been a nice visit. But I have to be at work early tomorrow so I'm going to have to say goodnight."

"Okay," I paused, not wanting to leave.

"Sure."

"Well, thanks for the conversation," I continued, still not making it out the door.

"Certainly."

"I'll see you in a couple of days," I finished as she nudged me out with a tap on the shoulder. And with that I went home for the night.

I was too humiliated to fully take in all that Elizabeth had said, and at the same time too elated from seeing her to care, but with each passing day her words would make more and more sense to me. Still, enough of her conversation sank in on the way home that I reached there with one troubling question on my mind. And since I wasn't above some fast self-motivating tactics to make myself sleep better that night, I found it necessary to wake up Mr. Landauer.

"What is it Ballard?" he asked after hearing me clear my throat about fifteen times near his bedroom door.

"How are you, Mr. Landauer?" I started as innocently as possible.

"What?" he asked.

"Do you think that I have a good character?"

"What?"

"Do you think that I have a good character?" I said more slowly this time to make sure of his complete comprehension.

"Of course, I love your character."

"No, Mr. Landauer. Answer seriously. The question is not, do you like my personality, but do you think that I'm an upstanding, clear thinking, practical member of your community?"

"Uh. Well, in this moment Ballard, clear thinking wouldn't be my first choice."

"Well..." I conceded that one. "What about the other two?"

"You are definitely upstanding, even at this moment, at one in the morning -- when everyone else is sleeping, -- you are standing up. You are must definitely upstanding."

"Thanks," I said with a smile. I figured I'd better take what I could get, and with that I went to bed.

Chapter 29

The next morning I awoke with the same question in my mind. What did it really mean to have a good character? And more importantly, did I have a bad one? The day before I didn't even know what character was and now I was obsessed with the thought of it. To be sure, if Ed had said the same thing to me, I would have taken it as a joke. But since these words were from Elizabeth, they danced in my head to be viewed and reviewed over and over again.

I decided to bring my all-important question to the place where all-important answers are given. The poker table. I could always count on my fellow janitors to sort out the most intricate details of even the most ridiculous questions. All I would have to do was put an idea out there and I could count on them to beat it into the ground, while I sat back and listened and picked from the conversation whatever I thought worthwhile.

As we set up for that night's game, I brought everyone a cup of coffee with an extra smile and an extra "how's it going," and then sat down trying to look as natural as possible. I waited for a couple of minutes, and seeing that we had not started on any interesting topics, I made my move.

"David?" I asked. "What do you think of Ed's character?"

"What?" was pretty much everyone's response.

"Well, well" said Charley. "Ballard seems to have come with an agenda for tonight's entertainment."

"No, I have no agenda," I protested.

"Well, what do you care about my character then?" asked Ed, more than a little irritated.

"Oh, nothing. I was just trying to make small talk."

"Um, no," said Ed. "You are definitely up to something."

"Well, I could tell you a thing or two about Ed's character," said Lester.

"What character?" asked David, "The boy's been a trouble maker since day one! Character is exactly what he doesn't have. But don't worry Ed, that is what we like about you, anyway."

"Ballard," insisted Ed, "who said what, about me?"

"No one has said anything about you Ed, it was just a simple question, no malicious intent involved. I could have easily asked about Lester, or David's character."

"But you didn't, you asked about mine."

"And I'm really sorry for it now."

"Well despite what you've heard, I'm not a bad person. I used to get in trouble as a kid but it wasn't about being a problem, it was just about trying to have some fun. You know this is a small town and sometimes you just have to make up things to do. It's true that I was an instigator but I never got anyone hurt, and I never hurt anybody. It was all just immature kid's stuff. Nothing serious, you know. So we egged some houses, and wrote phone numbers on bathroom walls, I can't believe that after ten years people still won't give it a rest!"

"Ed," I said trying to calm him down. "I'm truly sorry. I didn't mean to get into anything like this. I was just trying to be slick and bring up my own character. I just wanted to see what you all thought of me. I've never heard one bad thing about you and wouldn't have believed it even if I had."

"I knew it," said David. "Since when has anyone ever cared about my opinion? Asking me, that was your first mistake."

"Yes," said Charley, "but now I'm really curious how all this came up. Who said what about you, Ballard?"

"No, I was just thinking that maybe I wasn't the best guy, you know. I'm always a little moody, and all."

"Ballard?" asked Ed. "You are going to have to spill the beans now. What's up, man? Who said what? Huh? Who said what?"

"No, it's not a big deal or anything, it's just that Elizabeth had mentioned yesterday--"

"Elizabeth?" asked Ed.

"Yesterday?" asked Charley.

"Yeah." I said.

"But you didn't mention any of this yesterday," noted Charley.

"Well, she hadn't said it yet." And that was it. All of their mouths dropped open, and I knew that I was in real trouble now.

"You are a dog," said Lester. "I didn't know that you two were all that close!"

"No, it's not like that," I said.

"Like what?" asked Ed. "You went over to Elizabeth's house last night, after leaving here. No, we shouldn't suspect anything from that." They were all wide-eyed and eager to hear the whole story. I'd never seen them sitting so straight in their chairs before. Even Steven was motioning for me to open up.

"Please," I said, "it is nothing like that."

"Just tell us," said Charley, "where the issue of character came up and then we'll be much more able to answer your question. Because right now your asking about character is leaving you looking a little suspect."

"Oh, I can answer it now," said David. "You have absolutely no character at all whatsoever."

"You're a dog!" laughed Lester.

"You're lucky that her parents are in Costa Rica," continued David. "But that Mr. Cheswick might also have a thing or two to say about your character!"

"You are a dog!" again yelled Lester.

"Oh how I wish that I could still be a dog!" said David.

I realized that there was no way out, and to save Elizabeth's reputation I told the whole embarrassing story. They loved every bit of it, however, and their fun took some of the sting off of my humiliation. Charley, for one, seemed very impressed with Elizabeth.

"That girl really has a good head on her shoulders," said Charley.

"Oh, does she ever!" said David sarcastically.

"No, not to look at, David, but she really has a philosophical mind. That kind of insight is not there for everybody. She really has the strength of character to put Ballard in his place and at the same time to have made him a better person for it."

"So now do you still want to know if we think you have a good character?" asked Lester.

"No," I answered.

"Well let me just say that..."

"You're a dog!" Lester, David and Ed laughed out together.

"Thanks, guys," I said.

"You see," said Charley, "it isn't that you have bad character, because you don't, it's just that you are a little naïve. But don't worry, with a little bit of help from your friends, you are quickly growing out of that." They all laughed and I had to smile. I was certainly fortunate to have friends such as these, ever willing to laugh at the errors of my ways.

Chapter 30

We'd heard his voice echoing through the building for a few minutes before he'd found us working, so that wasn't the surprise. It was Saul's appearance rather than his visit that was most shocking. His face was pale and his eyes were bloodshot. He'd developed bags under his eyes that told of his recent late nights. His hair was uncombed and there seemed to be a sour odor coming from his body. He was dressed simply in blue jeans and tennis shoes, with his button down shirt hanging out haphazardly and wrinkled. Still, Saul stood tall with his head high and proud and his usual casual smile, as if nothing were out of the ordinary.

He walked with us as we worked, making small talk, and telling us about his latest readings and the works he was himself compiling. He explained about a book he was writing on the place of religion in society. He went on at length about some local politics, of which I didn't care anything for. Something about wasted money and water projects, but I didn't really follow it. I didn't want to seem rude though as I was happy for the company, so I just kept quiet, busying myself in my work, while Ed seemed to listen but carried a rather distant and strained look on his face. The whole conversation was really a blur in my mind until suddenly, in a strong voice, Ed spoke up.

"Listen, I know you better than anyone. What is it that you want to say? Whatever it is just spit it out." Ed seemed more serious than I had ever seen him. He was purposely trying to make his voice sound irritated, which didn't fit his character and was a little funny to me.

"No, I just felt like being with you guys tonight," Saul said with a laugh. "That's all. I just needed a guy's night out, you know, but you guys work late so it wouldn't have worked. Sometimes it can be lonely at home and I just wanted the company of friends. Seeing you guys really lightens my mind and puts me at ease. Besides, you haven't been by for awhile so I just wanted to say Hi."

"Yeah, I really wanted to say Hi also," I said, "but I never see you around town. I really wanted to thank you for inviting me to that play. It was a lot of fun. I really love your family. You're so blessed to all get along so well." Ed didn't seem to appreciate my comments at all and looked as if he were just waiting for me to shut up.

"Anyways, there's a reason you're here," pressured Ed. "And in all the years I've known you I've never seen you look so haggard. Your face is dirty and your clothes unkempt. What is going on with you? Or have you taken on my own fashion sense?"

Looking down at the ground, Saul appeared at first like he wasn't going to answer before saying, slightly above a whisper, "It's hard for me to talk about." He tried hard to keep the smile on his face, but he couldn't get it to conform and slowly he fell completely apart. He moved his hands as if explaining something to us but there were no words coming from his mouth. He seemed at once a completely pathetic creature.

"It's alright," I said, "you're among friends."

"I know it," continued Saul in the same low tone. "That's why I came here. You see... It's about Rachel."

"Did something happen to Rachel?" Ed asked suddenly worried.

"No. No. It's not like that. Not like that at all. I'm saying only that... Rachel has been... Well, she's been disappearing for long hours at a time and she won't tell me where or with whom she's been." Saul blurted this last part out in a sudden rush, as if he didn't want the words to spend too much time on his lips.

Hearing this, I remembered our day in the park when Saul for some reason wasn't invited. I figured that he still hadn't been informed, but didn't want to bring it up, as I didn't want to come between any struggles being waged between him and Rachel.

"So, what are you saying?" asked Ed.

"I think she's cheating on me."

"Cheating on you?" I stupidly asked. This was the last thing I expected to hear. I thought that maybe he was worried for her safety or worried about what she could be involved in, but the whole idea of his divorced wife cheating on him had never entered my mind.

"I know what you're thinking, but I love all of my exes. I care very deeply about their welfare and still have a great bond with them. Although we are no longer married, we all live for each other!"

"You mean that you live for them. But you can't expect them to live for you," said Ed.

"Why can't I expect that?" asked Saul. "Do you not live for your friends as well as your loved ones? I would do anything for them. They know that. My love for them has never decreased."

"But Saul," continued Ed, "you have no more rights with them. You divorced them, and now you have to accept them getting on with their lives."

"What is there to get on with? What more could she ask for? Have I not always been there for her? Have I not sheltered and protected her all these years? You can not say that our bond is any less serious because we no longer have the tie of marriage around it."

In my innocence, I couldn't believe what I was hearing. Was it possible that love could be reduced to this? I felt in that moment that Saul had fallen ill and didn't realize what he was saying.

"Are you sure she's seeing somebody?" I asked. "Maybe she just needs some time alone."

"Yeah, or maybe she has made some new friends," added Ed. "You never know with her. She's so very independent. I think she just needs to get out sometimes."

I felt that Ed was also trying to cover up for the park incident, and decided that I'd better tell the truth before this got out of hand. "If you're referring to some weeks ago, she was at the park with Elizabeth and me. We were just singing songs for our own amusement, but there was nothing romantic in it. I swear it."

Ed again gave me a disgusted look. "Ballard, he doesn't care about the park."

"I know about that," said Saul. "Rachel told me that you'd invited me, but she wanted to have fun and I somehow was not included in that equation. But it's more than that... She's been out everyday this week and when she comes home she has that look in her eyes that she used to have when she was with me. I never thought that she would be able to have those feelings for somebody else."

"But," I jumped in, "haven't you those feelings for three women?" I actually understood nothing about their situation, but I couldn't believe that Rachel was so conniving, and more than this, I didn't feel that it was any of his business even if she were. But I was fooling myself. They were a family, no matter how strange, and I had no right to jump to any conclusions about them. I started to feel as if I were talking out of place and resolved to hold my tongue.

"But..." started Saul in a weak voice.

"But what?" asked Ed. "Why not think of Rachel? How she must be feeling?"

"But," again pleaded Saul. But that was it. He broke down and started crying. Ed and I were speechless. He fell to the ground and curled up like a baby. It was a good half an hour before Ed was able to calm him down, and take him home. And I was left to wonder what was happening to my new family.

Chapter 31

"Knock, knock, knock! I'm here!" yelled a recognizable voice one morning. Upon first hearing his smooth, low toned voice, I felt I was flashing back in time. For a second I wasn't sitting in Mr. Landauer's kitchen, but was back in my own apartment in California. The last time I'd heard that voice was on a collect call paid me from his latest excursion to the Alameda County Jail, just to inform me of his incarceration, not to ask for any assistance. And still, I could hardly believe that someone from my old life had caught up to me. I thought it must be a mistake, a likeness that was uncanny.

I'd written to my Aunt Camille upon first moving in with Mr. Landauer, to let her know my address and that I was safe, so I shouldn't have been surprised to be hearing again from this man. However, seeing the face of my father on Mr. Landauer's doorstep produced nothing other than pure shock in me.

"Ballard, my boy! I'm so glad to see you," said my father in his usual overly boisterous voice. "Wow, you live in this house?" Entering the house on his own permission, he took everything in. "You've really stepped up in the world, haven't you? Who'd you have to scam to get into here? Boy, you always were a clever one weren't you?"

My father wormed his way around the front room in his usual fashion, merely talking but not wanting to have a conversation. He didn't care for my responses, but was only looking to hustle his way into this new situation. He never even considered that maybe he didn't have to scam his way into his own son's home. But, of course, he did, as I had no intention of letting him stay.

"When did you get out of jail?" I asked as dryly as I could, not wanting to show too much concern.

"About two weeks back. I talked to your aunt four or five days ago and she gave me your address here. I just wanted to see how my only son's doing and maybe stay a few days. It's really out of the way, isn't it? Is there much to do? It doesn't look like you've got any neighbors."

"The town is another three miles in."

Mr. Landauer, hearing the voices, came from his room, excited about the possibility of company.

"This is my friend and owner of the house, Mr. Landauer. And this is my father, Jeffery Davies."

"Oh?" asked Mr. Landauer. "Welcome, welcome. It's so nice to meet you, Mr. Davies. Would you like some tea or coffee?" On learning that this was my father, Mr. Landauer became very excited and set out immediately to get into his good graces. I doubted if Mr. Landauer had ever met someone like my father and didn't want to explain the situation to him.

"Sure. Please. I'll have some coffee," said my father as he sized up Mr. Landauer and realized he had an easy target.

"Just a moment." Mr. Landauer raced away to make us all coffee. He was so excited that we could hear him banging away in the kitchen, trying to prepare everything as quickly as possible. My father's eyes got really big and I could see his mind working on overload.

"This is quite a house. The old man is a bit eccentric, huh? Well, you look good. Have you gotten a job yet?"

"I'm a janitor."

"What! I didn't raise you to be a janitor."

"You didn't raise me at all."

"But you went to college," he persisted.

"I didn't finish school, but regardless it is a good job. It has lots of benefits to it. Besides, it's an honest living. And that's the most important part."

Luckily for both of us Mr. Landauer came back before the conversation could get out of control. My father and I never actually said anything new to each other. We just kept rehashing the same subjects over and over again. It always came down to the same basic points that he thought I was smart, which meant I should be wealthy, and that I thought he was smart, which meant he should be honest.

"Come into the kitchen. We can have coffee and talk," said Mr. Landauer as he took my father by the hand and led him to the kitchen table.

They hit it off right away. They told the histories of their families, both making up quite a lot. Mr. Landauer told about how he used to be the Mayor and how he'd won in a landslide victory. But he left out the part about running from the town a disgrace. And my father told about how he was the oldest son in a broken home and how he supported his mother and sister by working on the docks of San Francisco. Of course, he left out the part about finding solace in cocaine and not having time for his own son as he was too busy relaxing in jail for petty crimes. I didn't want to burst their bubbles, as Mr. Landauer seemed to be having such a nice time, so I just kept quiet and drank my coffee wondering all the while when this would end.

The two of them made plans to visit the town after I went to work, which was shocking to me, as I didn't know that Mr. Landauer was even willing to go into the town. Something about my father always made people happy to do what they weren't normally willing to. I started to think that maybe there could be some benefit for Mr. Landauer in knowing my father if it got him out of the house. If I'd been thinking clearly, I would've warned Mr. Landauer of my father's troubles. But, unfortunately for me, I said nothing and rushed off to work about five hours early.

I knew my father wouldn't steal anything from Mr. Landauer. He was more of the mooching type. His normal gig would be to stay around the house for as many months as possible, being happy for a roof over his head and something to eat. Of course, that's the same way I moved into the house and I had to laugh a bit to myself thinking that I was indeed my father's son.

When I arrived home that night, Mr. Landauer informed me that my father had gone back to California. He'd said that this town was too small for him and to give me his good-byes and tell me that he was glad I was doing well. I was glad he'd seen my home but was even more relieved he was gone. It was not like I hated him, but I knew that he was unable to keep himself out of trouble and I didn't want him to make all new enemies here.

At first I believed my father actually had a major breakthrough. I thought that maybe the innocence and honesty of Mr. Landauer had somehow caused him, for the first time, not to create any trouble. But over the next week the calls started coming in. First Mr. Cheswick let me know that my father had written a bad check for $54.56 to pay for Mr. Landauer and his dinner. I was at least impressed they'd visited the diner but later found out that Mr. Landauer had waited in my father's car while my father went in and ordered take-out. Then came a call from Martha's Designs, where my father had bought over $2,000 worth of clothes. Fortunately, my father put my name and address on the check just in case it didn't go through. Could that simple gesture be the beginning of an honest living? Then came the call from the junkyard where my father paid for a beat-up Chevy, to replace his beat-up Toyota. That only cost him, or I should say me, $600. Luckily for me, when all was said and done, my father hadn't spent more than the savings I'd accumulated over the past six months. I paid them all in full and started over again.

Chapter 32

I was awakened early one Sunday morning to the irritating thump of Issa tapping me on the head.

"Just like old times, right?" she said. "You look dead, and you wake up to my face and the sound of my thump!" She laughed happily. She seemed exceedingly proud of herself, but I only wondered what she was doing in my room at this early hour.

"What time is it?" I asked.

"It's seven o'clock."

"Seven! Hey, come on, this is my day off!" I yelled, rolling over to cover my face. I was happy to see her but the sluggishness of my sleep had not yet worn off, nor did I want it to.

"I know, but Elizabeth and I are going to Cloverdale today and she said that you would want to come."

"Oh! Great! Let's go!" All it took was that name, cherished of all names to me, to completely wipe away all traces of lethargy. I was so excited to hear that Elizabeth had thought of me and that we had a planned excursion for the day that I forgot everything else and jumped out of bed ready to hit the road.

"Um... Don't you want to take a shower and get dressed first?" Issa asked covering her mouth to keep from laughing.

"Oh, yeah!" I was still in my work clothes from the night before and could feel the drool covering my chin. "I'll just be a few minutes, okay?"

"Okay."

When I reemerged from the bathroom, I found Elizabeth and Issa trying to have coffee with Mr. Landauer. They'd convinced him to join us for our outing and he was busily packing things he thought we'd need while Elizabeth kept telling him she'd already prepared everything. After another twenty minutes of him packing and her unpacking, we all got into Elizabeth's car and headed for Cloverdale.

We drove the hour east to Cloverdale and anther half hour northward after getting off the highway. We were heading towards a remote area of the city that I hadn't researched while searching for the Costa Rican diner. This part of town was obviously older as the buildings were run down and the streets dirty. Eventually, we arrived on the outskirts of a huge forest. All we could see till the horizon in both directions were trees. The sun was out and appeared to be casting a glow all around the forest. I don't know if it was due to the fact that I hadn't seen a forest in so long, or anything more than Daisy's tree for that matter, but the area seemed almost magical to me. Maybe it was the fact that these trees were obviously hundreds of years old and had paid witness to so many generations of people and creatures.

"We're here," said Elizabeth.

"My God," I said. "I was beginning to think that they didn't have trees in this part of the country."

"I've never seen anything this beautiful," exclaimed Mr. Landauer. "These trees are so old. Just imagine everything they've seen. They must have been here since the Sioux Indians inhabited these parts. It's truly extraordinary, when you think about it."

"It really is beautiful here," said Elizabeth. "It reminds me so much of my village in Costa Rica. The mountains there are covered in old forests."

"So?" asked Issa. "Are we going in?"

We parked the car, gathered up our supplies and headed straight into the heart of the forest. There was no path and I began to wonder if we were heading any place in particular. The forest began to get thick and the light started to fade.

"Do you think there's any poison oak here?" I asked.

"Well," said Elizabeth, "there's red oak, and bur oak, there's elms and pine trees, there's red cedar and cottonwood. But poison oak... I've never had a problem with it, but can't say for sure. Don't worry, though, there's a clearing up ahead, with just plain grass."

We walked in silence for another twenty minutes. We each tried to take in the magnitude of the beauty before us. There was a purity in the air, in the sights, in the dirt, that was undeniable. The calmness of our surroundings had an unquestionable effect on us. I felt as if my mind had actually slowed down and was not being beaten by the usual array of thoughts constantly passing through it.

Eventually, the forest opened up into a giant field at least a hundred yards in diameter. Only the blue sky could be seen above. We were completely alone. All of the chirpings of civilization were gone and only the sounds of our breathing could be heard. We spread out our blankets and prepared some cheese sandwiches. Although we were happy to be together, the magnitude of the moment kept us from talking. We ate in silence and just enjoyed being there. I was so happy that Mr. Landauer was able to experience this. I could see that he, most of all, was touched by the event.

"It's so beautiful," quietly ventured Mr. Landauer, as if not to disturb anything.

"You know, Grandma Daisy used to play here as a kid," said Elizabeth.

"Really?" asked Issa. "It's funny to even think of her as a kid. I can't even picture it. What was she like then?"

"She hasn't talked much about it except to say that in those days her only care in the world was getting to this spot unseen, as the forest was surrounded by white-only neighborhoods. This being the case, she used to sneak here in the early mornings, before dawn, and then stay until after nightfall. She used to sit out here all day and just talk to the sky. She said she always felt that something was out there listening to her. She didn't know what. She said there was some kind of vibration in this place and she used to just lie here for hours soaking it in."

"So she's the one who told you to come here?" I asked.

"Yes. She told me about this place when I first started coming to see her. I was sad all the time, and she said that if I came here everyday and just sat with my eyes closed, trying to commune with the spirit of the forest, I would slowly regain my peace of mind. And she also suggested that I bring back the branches that had fallen from the trees to use to light a fire next to her. Can you believe that in all those years before I'd come, no one had ever thought to light a fire there? She made do with the blankets that different women had brought her. Don't ask me how she survived."

"I don't understand how she's still surviving," I said.

"She's definitely a special one," added Mr. Landauer. "I guess that I just couldn't handle the fact that I always felt she could read my mind. That's what really scared me away from her."

"But, that's exactly what makes her special," answered Elizabeth. "Because you don't want to think anything negative in front of her, you automatically become a better person. She forces us to control our thoughts instead of letting our thoughts control us. That's the beauty in what she offers us."

Out of nowhere, seemingly in response to Elizabeth's words, arose a soft humming sound. At first it was barely audible, and I must have thought it was a bird or something. But then it slowly grew louder and I knew that we all heard it as we all stopped talking. It is wrong actually to call it a hum, as it was not a human or animal sound at all. It was more like a drone of the wind. It wasn't coming from anywhere in particular, but was completely surrounding us. Issa and Elizabeth both closed their eyes and simply took in the sound, but Mr. Landauer and I were suddenly shaken, as this was completely inexplicable. It must have shown on our faces, for after some time Issa touched both our hands and said, "It's alive here," and smiled.

Neither Mr. Landauer nor myself seemed interested in arguing this point. We instead sat as coolly as possible trying to finish our sandwiches. The drone grew steadily louder until I felt that it was coming from inside of me and the air became so thick that I felt as if I were submerged in water.

"Elizabeth," whispered Mr. Landauer, "what is this place? Have you brought us to meet our death? Don't forget that I'm an old man, and easily frightened."

"Don't worry," said Elizabeth. "It's a holy spot. Men have worshiped here for thousands of years, knowing that here the voice of God could be easily heard. Grandma Daisy's own grandmother used to hold prayer services here with the women of Kent, the neighboring city. They used to come here to commune with the great Goddess. The nature is so alive that you can feel it touching you and speaking to you."

Though she said it in such a sweet and gentle way, Mr. Landauer -- and myself, I hate to say -- were not so easily soothed.

"But what is the sound?" asked Mr. Landauer.

"It's the sound of the Universe," said Elizabeth.

"Daisy calls it the Hum of the Mother," added Issa.

"The Mother?" I asked.

"Before there was anything in creation," said Elizabeth, "it is said that this sound was there."

"And when all of creation again is destroyed," continued Issa, "the hum will remain."

Mr. Landauer's eyes seemed to sink into his head as we sat there. He remained silent, but I was sure that his brain was on overload. As for my own mind, I just tried to hold my breath until Elizabeth would say that it was okay for us to leave. I didn't understand what was going on, and I was sure that nothing in my life had prepared me for this. I wanted answers but I had no idea what the questions were.

After a few more minutes the drone died down and the quiet of the forest again pervaded everything. None of us were ready to talk. While Issa and Elizabeth were in a meditative state, Mr. Landauer and myself were now more than willing to leave. Fortunately for us, no more sounds came.

On the way home no one talked. We were all lost in our own experience and no one was ready to ruin or forsake the experience of the others in order to express their own feelings. But for Mr. Landauer and myself, it was clear that the world had suddenly grown in potential and would never quite be the same.

Chapter 33

"Yes, I've heard a lot about your past," I told Mr. Landauer. "But I don't believe most of it. It's just a bunch of gossip from people with nothing better to do." I wasn't sure why Mr. Landauer was suddenly ready to talk about his past, this morning, but figured it had something to do with the previous day's experience in the forest.

"Well, Ballard, you might as well believe it because most of it is probably true."

"How could it be true?" I asked.

"Why shouldn't it be?"

"Most of the things they say are so absurd and clearly not within the realm of your personality."

"When you get to be my age, you too will have changed. Our experiences make us what we are today. Let me just tell you my story so that you won't have to wonder any longer."

"You don't have to."

"No, but I want to." Mr. Landauer eased into his seat and sipped some of his coffee. "You see, my life was so public. I was a politician. A great politician! But my confidence turned to arrogance somewhere along the way. Possibly fairly early on. At any rate, I reached a point where I really believed I could do no wrong, because of the simple fact that I usually did have all the answers. I didn't even have to try. All the correct things just seemed to pop into my head. I came to think that just because I thought of it, it must be right."

"Well, that hasn't changed," I laughed.

"No. But now I can at least listen to others, whereas before I only pretended to. Somehow, I managed to squander half the fortunes of this town on clearly ludicrous business dealings. But that isn't what changed me. It was the day when my wife packed up and left me to be with someone half her age. Some trucker just passing through town. That's when I realized I'd become so self-absorbed that I couldn't even see what was happening right in front of me. From my point of view, I loved her so much that I thought we didn't even need to make a show of it. That it was so apparent. But from her point of view, she was drying up in the heat of my arrogance. Her love for me just withered away.

"Losing her caused me to shut down. And in that shutting down I could clearly see how the town felt about me. They hated me. They hated my policies. They hated my power. They hated my very essence.

"Well, that was just too much for me to bear. I tried hard to change. My arrogance fell away easily but as it was such a dramatic shift, the town mistook my newfound kindness for dumbness. They thought I was losing my mind. The more they berated me, the more I really felt I was indeed going crazy. And the fact that I couldn't escape the town's ridicule led to a complete nervous breakdown, where as I told you before, I ended up running through the streets as naked as a newborn. And that was my lasting legacy.

"So my son, before he died, found me this place. But my grandson could never look me in the eye again. Saul had always looked up to me. I had given him his first real job in my administration, and he had defended me until the end. But when I lost it, he just didn't want to have anything to do with me anymore. And when his father died of a heart attack, he blamed me. Rightfully so."

There was a moment's silence before he asked me, "So what do you think?"

"Well," I thought for a moment. "I think after all that you came out just about perfect."

Pausing to raise his eyebrows, "Hey, what do you mean, *just* about?"

Chapter 34

I had not yet begun to process what happened that weekend in the forest, though I figured I would have plenty of time to contemplate the events while at work. That being the case, I struggled not to think about anything before reaching the mental laboratory of my job. The great thing about janitorial work was that my mind was free to explore whatever subjects were most pressing to me. And this evening, the hum of the forest was definitely on my agenda.

When I arrived that night, Lester told me that Ed had called in sick and that I would have to clean the high school on my own. I was more than ready to work alone, as it gave me more time to think. Plus, the added work would give me an excuse not to show up for cards, and I just wasn't in the mood that evening.

I didn't think Ed's absence was anything serious, until around 11:00 p.m., when I got a knot in my stomach, as if warning me of some impending trouble. For some reason I felt as if something bad were about to happen or had already happened. I awaited the bearer of bad news.

At around 11:30, when I was nearly finished with my work, I noticed a pair of eyes down the hall peering into the classroom at me. The eyes were just staring at me and apparently had been for some time.

"Who's there?" I called, a little freaked out. Although the school was always dark, I never felt scared because the town was so peaceful. But after the past weekend's events I was not in the mood for any more surprises. There was no answer, however, to my call.

"Who's there?" I yelled with a little more authority, hoping to scare the person, if they indeed were where they shouldn't be. Still there was no response, and my nerves became more on edge.

"Ed! Is that you? Stop playing around!"

"Ha!" came a sudden loud and extremely angry response. "Don't try and pretend like you don't know where he is, Ballard! You know! You know!" It was Saul, and he was now rushing towards me. I wasn't sure what was going on, but as he got closer it looked as though he was going to hit me, so I put my arms up to cover my face.

"Don't cover your face! You are going to talk to me!" Saul had stopped about two feet from me and was boiling with rage. His face was bright red, his clothes were disheveled and his breath reeked of days of neglect.

"You tell me where that friend of yours is!"

"Saul, calm down. I don't know what you're talking about."

"Of course you know! Of course you know! You must have been in on it together."

"Saul," I said as calmly as I could with his face inching ever closer to mine. "You are going to have to calm down and tell me what's going on, because I truly have no idea."

"That animal!" he screamed, finally moving from me and taking to pacing around the classroom. "That lying animal! Can you even imagine what he's done? Can you even imagine what that no good cheat, look-me-in-the-face-and-smile-while-you-rip-my-life-away wretch has done?"

"What is it? You're talking about Ed? You're talking about Ed in this way? As far as I know, he is sick at home. What's going on?" I tried to get him to sit down but he was not at all interested. I don't think he even saw me after he started pacing; it was just my presence that was allowing him to say what he needed to say.

"Never in my life," continued Saul, with one hand waving and the other running again and again through his hair. "Never in my life have I met such a scoundrel as this. Maybe read about them. Yes, I might have read about such people, but never did I imagine that one would waltz their way into my life and destroy what was most precious to me?"

"What is it, Saul?" I asked again in earnest, now a little scared at what his answer might be.

"That man has stolen my wife. He's stolen the true love of my life. I know that I've had many loves, but me and her... How could he do this to me? How could she do this to me? My God! How could you do this to me?"

"Saul? Sit down. Start from the beginning. Because I'm sure that you can't be saying what it sounds like you're saying." I was extremely confused now and my head started racing, trying to imagine before he told me, what exactly was going on. As far as I knew Ed was always extremely open and honest with me, a true friend who would tell me everything good or bad, and I couldn't have imagined he would have kept something of this magnitude a secret.

I pushed a chair towards Saul, which he grabbed and threw across the room. So I smartly backed up and asked him again, "Saul, start from the beginning because I'm a little lost here."

"What, man?" yelled Saul finally looking me straight in the eye. "Have you not been listening to what I'm saying? That rat stabbed me in the back! He acted like a friend! For so many years I thought that he was a friend and all this time he was just setting me up so he could rip my life apart!"

"Saul, shut up for a second!" I yelled. "If you have something to say then just calm down and say it!"

My words were like a sudden shock, and there followed an abrupt moment of silence. Saul put both hands up as if he were going to start explaining logically what was going on, but when he opened his mouth no words came out. He stared at me for a moment and I gave him all the time he needed. He took a huge breath and let out a long sigh. He then hung his head and looked as if he didn't want to talk anymore, he just kept shaking his head back and forth while seemingly pleading with the floor.

Eventually, he reached into his pants pocket and slowly pulled out a single piece of paper.

"Read this," he said finally in a semi-normal, if not choked up voice.

It was a letter:

To My Dearest Saul,

After reading this letter I'm sure you will not want to hear anything about being my dearest from me. You are, though, very dear to me Saul. This is the truth. But more than this is the fact that I need to start living my own life. As much as I adore you, I cannot live with you anymore. I know that you cannot understand this and that is why I'm leaving you this note. It is the easiest way for me to get my point across, and move on. And whether or not you understand, you will be forced to accept it. It is the choice that I have made.

Ed and I have decided that we need to try and make something out of our talent. It is better that we barely survive playing at bars in a big city than to waste away playing in parks in this town. We may never make a lot of money with music or achieve any amount of fame or success, but we owe it to ourselves to try and live out our dreams. More than this, so much more than this, is the simple fact that we are in love. I know that you feel as though you still love me, and that in some way I belong to you, but I am not yours and haven't been for a long time. I must continue my life in my own way. I owe it to myself. I owe it to you. Please forgive me and please forgive Ed.

Your friend forever,

Rachel

I folded the letter up and handed it back to Saul. I was completely shocked, as I had no idea that the two of them had any feelings for each other. Looking back on things it made sense to me, but still in the moment I couldn't help feeling that Ed had abandoned me as well.

I shook my head for a long time and had to sit down. Eventually Saul also sat down. I didn't know what to say to him. I felt loyal to Ed, sorry for Rachel, and not very empathetic towards Saul. But in that moment, we were bound by our common shock. In that moment, I felt extremely sorry for what we had lost, while remaining angry that Ed would do such a thing without telling anybody.

"I'm sorry Saul," I eventually managed to say. "But maybe she's right."

"How can this be right?" he asked.

"Not the action, but the reason," I said. "She did need to move on. You are not married anymore, and you just have to accept it."

"I don't know how I can go on living like this," he said putting his head in his hands. "If I knew where they went I'd go after them. What else do I have to live for?"

"Saul! Don't be crazy. You have Issa. How can you go running after someone who doesn't love you, when you have a daughter who needs you?"

Saul merely shook his head as if he couldn't understand, or didn't want to understand, what I was saying.

"No! I must find her," he repeated to himself.

"Saul!" I now said with disgust. "Did you hear what I said! You have a daughter. She should mean everything to you, not Rachel.

Remembering what Elizabeth had said to me that day at her house, I continued, "You have to think clearly about this and look at the big picture. Right now you are wallowing in self-pity, but if you don't look at the big picture then you could lose much more than your ex-wife."

Like on his previous visit, Saul broke down and started crying. I then remembered the day that Ed told me that Saul would one day fall off his pedestal and realized that today was that day. I wondered how long Ed could have been planning this. I wanted to believe that it was a rash, spur of the moment thing, but in light of his previous statements and Mr. Cheswick's warning to look out for Ed, I just wasn't sure anymore.

I took Saul home that night, as he'd walked all the way to the school. Issa was there waiting on the steps, but she didn't look at him nor did he look at her. After Saul had entered the house, Issa walked over and gave me a hug.

"Can you believe this?" she asked.

"I can't."

"I suspected for a long time that they were in love," she said. "I knew that they at least enjoyed each other's company. But I never thought that they would just run off and leave us all to wonder and to worry over them. They think they can just start over and it won't affect us. But actually, we all are going to have to start over."

What more could I add? She had said all there was to say, so I stood there silently.

"I only hope that one day Rachel will return," continued Issa. "That is all I ask. To see her one more time in this life. I don't even need to ask her why, because I can understand why. I only wish that I had had the opportunity to say good-bye. She should have at least given us that. Then I wouldn't have held any of this against her. Then I would have been completely fine and even agreeable with it. But now she has left us like this. And poor Father might never recover." With that, she said good-bye and went inside. Dejected and resigned, I returned home and went to bed.

Chapter 35

Mr. Landauer, upon hearing of Saul's troubles, insisted on going to Saul's home immediately. I urged him to wait some time, however, thinking it would be better to give Saul a chance to recover before giving him the added shock of Mr. Landauer's visit. So we decided to wait one week before going over, which turned into one week of hell for my old friend. Mr. Landauer was unable to sleep, contemplating only on what that visit might bring. It would be much more than a check-up, it would be a long overdue family reunion. When the morning finally arrived, we were both a little nervous, as we hadn't heard anything from the family.

"Maybe they've moved past this," I offered.

"Not likely," said Mr. Landauer. "For all of Saul's problems, his greatest problem, which can at times be his finest asset, is his passion and his persistence, or rather his persistence of his passions. Once he digs his mind into something, it is hard to get him to sway from it. I don't think he'll give up on Rachel so easily."

I stood in the doorway waiting to leave but Mr. Landauer kept looking around the house for something. Confused I finally asked him, "What are you looking for?"

"I can't remember," he said.

"Then, let's go."

"But what if I need it?"

"Then we'll come back for it," I said. I'd never seen Mr. Landauer this nervous over anything. After one more look through the entire house, he finally made his way to the car.

We were completely silent the whole drive there. I wasn't sure if he was more worried about what he should say to Saul or about what Saul would say to him. I also wondered if Saul would become angry with me for bringing his grandfather over. But I decided it was definitely time for them to meet face to face, and since Saul was already experiencing difficult times, we might as well let him suffer it all at once.

When we reached the house and rang the doorbell, we heard a loud noise coming through the house before the door flew open. With wild and expectant eyes Saul stared at us, hoping beyond hope. A moment passed, and then realizing who was standing before him, his face turned sour, and the tears again welt up.

"What are you doing here? Do you want to torment me or laugh at my pain?"

"No, I only want to be a comfort to you." Mr. Landauer squeezed Saul's shoulder. Saul, not having any fight left, shook his head before turning around and wandering off in silence.

Mr. Landauer and I didn't know what to do. The door was only halfway open and we weren't sure whether or not we should venture in. Eventually, Issa peeked out the door.

"Oh. Ballard, Mr. Landauer," she said in a very subdued tone. Her eyes were red from crying and her clothes were wrinkled, looking slept in.

"Can we come in?" I asked.

She slowly opened the door and what we found was more than we could have imagined. There were broken vessels, clothes and papers littered all over the floor. As we walked through the house, we saw that every framed photo and work of art had been torn from the walls and many bookcases and shelves had been ripped apart. In the living room, we saw Saul sitting at the piano poking at the notes, while Emma tried to get him to drink some water. We could see through a passageway that Amber was busying herself cooking something.

Emma looked up and rushed over to us. "Grandfather," she said, giving him a hug. "Thank you, both of you, for coming. Saul is inconsolable. He can't see me, he can't see Amber, and he can't even see Issa. He just mopes around, followed by periodic outbursts of violence."

Hearing the talking, Amber had walked into the room. "Mr. Landauer," she said surprised. "It's so good to see you. It's been so long."

"That it has."

"I never really got to know you, but I've heard all about you from Issa and Ballard." She was trying hard to act normal and put on a friendly face despite the destroyed house.

"Would you like some coffee? We were just about to sit down for breakfast."

"Sure. I could use it."

Issa had hidden away somewhere, so that left the four of us to sit at their big dining room table. I couldn't help but remember the last time I'd sat here and how lively it had been. Now we tried to talk in a nice way, Mr. Landauer and I feeling it was our duty to show our support for them by giving them some semblance of normalcy for at least this brief moment.

"How long has he been like this?" Mr. Landauer asked.

"All week," said Emma.

"That night after Ballard brought Saul home," started Amber, "for a moment, there was some hope. He seemed resigned to the situation. Pathetic still, but at least accepting. But the next morning Saul woke up screaming and yelling and tore this whole house apart. The cook and the maid both left. What could they do? They were also scared."

"And Issa?" I asked.

"Poor Issa," Emma said taking my hand in hers. "Issa just cries all day. She keeps her head in her books pretending as if she's studying but her eyes are always red and puffy. She is so strong and can't understand how a grown man can be reduced to this. She doesn't want to accept it. But every time we walk into the living room, we are forced to accept it. Even we are tired. As you can see, we haven't even cleaned up the mess around here. It all feels so pointless now."

"But we can't put up with this much longer," said Amber. "We want to help him, and give him time but we are also planning to leave. For Issa's sake and for our own. What can we do with him if he won't even try? If he won't even move. And if he becomes violent again?"

"His love has completely blinded him," I said.

"Love?" asked Amber. "What love is in it? What love was ever in it? It's simply a selfish attachment. It's a selfishness so strong it's killing him. What love was ever really in it?"

"But you used to love him too, right?" I asked.

"What is real love?" she continued. "I mean real, selfless, unconditional love? Can you imagine that we ever had anything that was unconditional here? No, Ballard, all love rests on what we can get out of the relationship. I loved my husband because I thought he cared so greatly for me. I thought he adored me. I thought he worshipped me. But then I came to find out that he had two previous wives, and suddenly my love turned from divinely ordained, to worthless miscalculation. How can that happen?"

I just shook my head.

"It can't happen," said Amber. "It can't happen if it's real love. Love is the feeling you have for someone else's kids, not your own. It is pure appreciation for their existence, without attachment, and without desire. But who can care for someone else's kids as much as their own? Especially if those kids are ugly and rowdy!"

"Amber, you're so depressing," said Emma dryly.

"What is depressing in it?" asked Amber. "That's life. These are the plain and simple facts of life."

"But what is the world without love?" I asked.

"Ballard..." she took her time looking at me in earnest. "Love is an ideal. I hate to say it because Saul would have said it, but it's true. I so believe that love is just an ideal. If you care enough to work towards it, then you may truly be happy one day. But as for me? I'm too tired. Too tired to try anymore."

We tried to finish the lunch that Amber had cooked, but none of us were really hungry. Eventually we gave up and walked back into the living room. Amber went over to Saul and pushed him really hard, but he just simply caved into the piano and said nothing.

"Get up! Get up you stupid man! Look at the family you have left! You stupid man!" Amber could not help herself and broke down in tears. Saul slowly got up and walked away to his bedroom.

"We've all reached our limit," said Emma trying herself not to cry.

"Is there anything we can do?" asked Mr. Landauer.

"Coming here was enough. We really appreciate your support. There's a doctor coming this afternoon, but I really doubt that he can do anything. Only time is going to heal this."

Emma walked us to the door and thanked us again for coming. Two weeks later the three girls had all moved into Emma's parents' house, and within the month to their own apartment.

Chapter 36

Although I'd seen Elizabeth at least four days a week for nearly half a year, and had engaged her in hours of useless conversation, I began to feel that maybe I was alone in my adoration. Amber's talk on love had left me wondering whether love was indeed nothing more than selfish attachment. I started to look at little things - like the sparkle in my eyes that did not appear to be in hers. It wasn't that she wasn't nice to me, because she was always there to be a comfort for my endless need for entertainment, but I started to feel that I wasn't more than just a friendly face to her. I started to wonder if I was just making up this relationship between us, or if worse still she was of Amber's opinion that there was no such thing as real love. Saul's situation showed me just how much we could truly be a victim of our own imaginings -- not seeing the world for what it was. I became determined to find out the exact nature of Elizabeth's feelings for me.

With this in mind, I nervously walked into the Café early one dark morning, hoping to hear Elizabeth tell me I was being a silly fool, that of course she loved me more than life itself. I waited to get her attention, and then asked her if we could talk. She looked at me rather seriously, as if she didn't know what was coming. I just nodded my head in affirmation of nothing and took my seat. After a few moments, she came and sat across from me.

"So..." she slowly started. "What's up? It must be something serious as you don't have your normal dorky grin or amusingly determined walk."

I didn't smile, which caused her smile to fade, and she just looked at me and waited for what was to come. I could see her brain working as if she were putting together possible answers for whichever question was about to come. "There's no need to be shy here. Just tell me what you want to say."

"Well, you know the situation with Saul?"

"Yes, it's heartbreaking. Issa told me all about it." She paused for a second, unsure of what I was getting at. "It's sad but it was only a matter of time till that house broke up. They're all such different people."

"Well, that basically brings me to the question I have for you. Which, incidentally, is not easy for me to ask, so if you would stop looking me in the eyes for just a moment, it would make it a bit easier."

She smiled. "Just tell me what it is you need to say."

I considered my options, but decided that all I could do was be honest and put everything out there. "I have to know, Elizabeth, if I've been fooling myself these last few months with my endless fantasies about our relationship."

"Fooling yourself?" Her face became more serious as she looked towards the ground, squirming slightly in her seat.

"For the last few months," I started, "I've been able to think of nothing but you. I've fallen hopelessly in love with you. Until recently, I was sure you also felt the same way about me. But what reason do I have to assume that? I realize now that I don't know you as well as I thought I did. I just have to know if you even believe in love? I know it sounds like a funny question, but I had a talk with Amber the other day. She said she doesn't even believe in love. But more importantly, whether you believe or not, I must know what your feelings are for me. I'm putting myself completely out there, so you should at least be honest and up front with me." As I finished, Elizabeth took my hand and I realized that what she was about to say was going to be very hard for me to hear.

"Ballard. I'll always be honest with you. This is something that I've thought a lot about. Not just our situation, but love in general. I do believe in love. I have dedicated my life to love. I can see no greater purpose in this world than love. That is why I'm studying psychology, and want to work with children."

For a fleeting second I felt there was some hope.

"But not this kind of love."

And the hope was gone forever.

"The kind of love that you speak of is an exclusive love. But love can't be exclusive. What you're talking about is a comfort level. When it is there it makes us feel secure, happy, wanted, but when it is gone it causes our minds to lose all control and fall into helpless depression. And those people that we supposedly loved yesterday, we hate the next day. That just can't be real love. That is merely passion. I've finally gained control of my life after too many years of depression, and to love again, to love in this way, would be to give up that control over who I am. I cannot believe that this kind of love is pure. The only real love is the love we feel for people like Daisy. Because that is the only kind of selfless love which we keep whether Daisy talks to us or not, feeds us or not, plays with us or not. We know that Daisy is there for everyone and not just us, and we don't mind it. In fact we accept it and it inspires us. This is the only love that I can believe in. I'm sorry."

In one instant, I was crushed beyond repair. I knew she was grateful for my friendship, but to imagine a life where more wasn't possible with the one whom I cherished so – it was not a life I wanted. In that moment, I knew I never wanted to have these kinds of feelings for another person. At the same time, I didn't want to admit that what I felt was merely the sway of attachment - a comfort level. While sitting there with Elizabeth, I made a vow that from then on, I would never give my heart to another but would save it forever for the one I'd dedicated it to. I decided that I would not be pulled again by temptations and for the first time I felt as though I would control my mind and make it do what I wanted it to.

Before I could control my mind however, I would have to control my tears. I was now even more embarrassed than could be imagined. I told Elizabeth that I was sorry for any discomfort I'd caused her and hoped she would never forget this friend, as I would never forget her. I then got up as gracefully as possible and left the shop. I walked slowly, giving Elizabeth the chance to stop me. But she didn't. She let me go.

To my horror, as I stepped out the door, my face drenched in tears, I tripped over Ruben Bennet, standing there with his friend Phiser Mitchell.

"Oh, be careful my boy," said Mr. Mitchell. "Ruben's an old man you know."

"Yes I know. I'm sorry," I stuttered.

"What do you mean, '*you know!*'" joked Ruben. "I'm not so old!"

Then, seeing my face, they eased up a bit and tried to give consoling pats on my back. But all I could think of was how to run away.

"Well now," said Mr. Bennet "I think he's finally ready."

"Give the boy a break, Ruben."

"Don't worry, son. For the first time I'm happy when looking in your eyes because I know you're headed in the right direction. There is no worse feeling than being completely broken down, but we never seem to move forward until that day when we renounce all control. So for you I'm exceedingly happy."

"He said the same thing to me the day after I married his sister!" laughed Mr. Mitchell. "And though it was no joke then, I can truly say now that it was the best thing that ever happened to me. Because, for the first time in my life, I had to surrender to someone else. I had to give up some part of myself. But in doing that I was forced to expand as a person."

"And to expand is tough," said Mr. Bennet.

"Yes, you either expand or you explode," continued Mr. Mitchell.

I wanted to yell at them that they didn't even know my situation, but I figured that it wasn't worth the effort. Later, I would realize just how well the words did indeed fit. But, for now, I wanted nothing more than to be alone. I wanted merely to wallow in self-pity and curse God for giving me a fate not worth a life.

"Ease up on yourself, kid," said Mr. Mitchell, "because no one else will."

"Yeah, especially me!" said Mr. Bennet. After a few more pats on my back, they finally let me be and I raced home to the comfort and solitude of my room.

Chapter 37

I remembered the words of Grandma Daisy telling that the one beast we needed to corral, we were completely helpless in controlling. I wondered how controlling my mind could have helped me with Elizabeth. It wouldn't have made her love me any more. It wouldn't have made me love her any better. The only thing I would have been able to control was letting myself become vulnerable. Was Elizabeth right -- that the only answer to keeping control was not to fall in love at all? I just couldn't understand how that could be the answer. I didn't want to think about that even being an option.

Daisy's words haunted my sleep that night, while Elizabeth's face haunted my waking. My heart ached from the loss of a girl who was never mine. Was I crazy? Perhaps it was just the human condition. That, of course, would've been an easy out but Daisy's assurance to a purpose and goal of life left me unable to accept that answer. I didn't know why I accepted Daisy's words as even legitimate, but I had an unexplainable faith in her simply because she seemed to have mastered life. I'd never really developed any relationship with Daisy apart from Elizabeth, and decided this was the time to start one.

I went to see her an hour before the start of my work, so that I would have the good excuse of getting to work on time if I needed a convenient reason for getting away. Also, I knew that Elizabeth wouldn't be there at that time, and I thought it would be best, or at least more comfortable for the both of us, if I didn't show my face around her for some time. As I neared Daisy I felt confident, thinking that this was the best thing for me to be doing. When Daisy saw my face, however, she looked at me rather suspiciously.

"Well now," she said, simply shaking her head knowingly.

"I've thought a lot about the things you've said," I started.

"Have you?" she asked, seemingly unbelieving. "Or could it be that what is a lot for you, and what is a lot for me, are not on the same scale?"

"Well... that could be the case," I said. She was playing with me, which was confusing, as I was for the first time coming to her in earnest.

"I don't want to become a slave to my mind," I told her, as if to prove that I'd heard something of what she'd said before. "I don't want to end up like Saul... Please, can you advise me on what I should do?"

Shaking her head, Daisy asked me, "Why do you act as if you're so dumb?"

And I admit that I was completely dumbfounded by this question.

"It is not," she continued, "as if you don't know what is right and what is wrong, but instead you simply choose what you know is wrong out of habit. You go on asking infinite questions like a fool when the simple answer in life is to just do what you know is right. I'm sick of seeing you like this. Stand up for yourself. If you want to become a good person, then it is up to you to make yourself into the person you want to be. You're not a feeble mouse having to run the course that life sets before you, but you are a mighty warrior able to choose if you want to turn right or turn left. But you will certainly suffer for your choices, so by God start making the right ones."

"But how do I know what is right and what is wrong?" I pleaded.

"You are not a fool. You know when you are making a decision if it is in the world's best interest or if it is purely rooted in your own selfish intentions."

"And my mind?" I asked.

"The mind is very complicated," she said. "It will hide and deceive you. It will pretend to be your friend only to capture hold of you and bring you once again into its powers. Are you sure you want to control it, or are you merely seeking to pacify it?"

"But Daisy, look at me," I told her, completely disgusted by my own pathetic state. "Don't I look like someone on his last leg?"

"Um... no, not really," she said. "You look like someone who is desperate to get back the illusions that were recently taken from him."

"I don't understand," I said. "Are you playing with me? Do you not want to talk with me?"

"I want nothing more than to talk with you," she said. "But I want you to want to hear what I have to say. Tell me, what has changed so drastically that you are now ready to believe? Tell me, who are you that I should believe?"

"What am I but a silly janitor that can barely support himself," I said, suddenly growing frustrated by the conversation.

"The question 'what am I,'" she started, "is dripping with all the superficiality of a high school lover. In a world of billions exactly like yourself, what does it really matter 'what' you are? A much more pressing question is 'who' you are."

"I'm Ballard."

"There have been great conquerors who have held millions under their control and they had the exact same problems as you. What does it matter if you are a great king, or famous musician with millions adoring your every movement, if you don't know who you are? But if you do know? For those who have answered this most pressing question, it didn't matter if they were rich or a beggar, for they were perfectly content and happy having unlocked the mysteries of the universe. Let every ring of the bells be a constant reminder of how far we've come and how far we need to go. Don't hide away from the fight, but embrace it as life's purpose."

"I want to conquer my mind," I said, "but I can't see how it's possible. I want to know the mysteries of the world, but what more can I do?"

"And what exactly have you done?" she asked. "Other than feel sorry for yourself, what exactly have you done?" She waited for me to answer but her tone made me feel that it wasn't wise, so I remained silent.

"Knowledge, like anything, comes with a price," started Daisy. "To get a little, you have to give a little. You want to know the mysteries of the universe? You are not even willing to give up your morning coffee. But to get the greatest gift, you must pay the highest price. To gain immortality you must give up your life. To gain an inexhaustible contentment, and a never-ending bliss, then you must give up your inexhaustible desires and your biting attachments."

"But haven't I given up my life to come here?" I questioned. "I gave up everything to come here. I just don't understand."

"You don't understand because you don't want to understand. First, the desire to know, to really know, must flourish in you and become all encompassing, and then all the other problems will fall away."

"But I do want to know," I pestered.

"Then hold on to that desire above all others."

Chapter 38

"It really appears that everyone's life is falling apart," said Mr. Landauer. "Well, except mine, but that's more because I don't have a life to have fall apart. See, Ballard, there are some benefits to being a boring old man."

"Mr. Landauer, there is nothing boring about you."

"I really thought that you and Elizabeth were going to make it, though."

"Make it?" I asked. "We didn't even start it."

"But you both seemed so happy."

"Sure, because in my head we were happy, and you only got the scoop from there. But it turns out that it was created, lived out, and destroyed all up there."

"Maybe that's why we get along so well. Because we both have active imaginations."

"Thanks."

"Well, at least there's one good thing about all this."

"What's that?" I asked.

"It can't get any worse."

"Hum... I was actually thinking that it can always get worse, so maybe I should be happy that it's only this bad thus far."

"Ah, so you have become a philosopher!"

"Well, at least a disappointed lover."

"That's exactly where we get all our philosophers, son. Every one of them!"

We both laughed at the absurdity of our situation. Two men separated by fifty years, wanting nothing more than love from the world, but no longer believing in it. I had left my family while his family had left him, and we seemed to be the only comforts for our lonely hearts.

One morning at about 9:00 a.m., there was a knock at the door. Mr. Landauer and I looked at each other with wonder, as we hadn't had any guests for a couple of months. Neither of us felt like getting up from our seats but eventually -- thinking that at least I was younger so had no excuse for being tired -- I got up and opened the door.

"Is my Grandfather here," he said in a subdued voice.

I couldn't believe what I was seeing. It was Saul, all cleaned up, looking rested and fully in control of himself. I just looked at him with surprise for a moment before he repeated his question to me.

"Of course. He's in the dining room," I said. Forgetting he'd never been to this house before, I neglected to show him where the dining room was and just watched him in awe as he tested all the doors before finally, coming to my senses, I took him into the kitchen.

Mr. Landauer looked up at Saul in complete disbelief, and Saul looked back without any kind of expectation on his face. And I looked from one to the other and back again, waiting for the happy reunion to begin. I was smiling so big that I made up for both of them, neither of whom seemed to be in control of their mouths and simply stared. Realizing that this was going to take some time, I backed up a little and tried to pretend I was making myself invisible, knowing full well that they could no longer see me.

"Grandfather?" whispered Saul.

Not being able to open his mouth, Mr. Landauer just stood up and put his hand on Saul's shoulder.

"Grandfather," started Saul again, shrinking slightly back towards the door. Mr. Landauer seemed confused and began looking around the room at all of the paintings of his family members. Looking towards the back of the room, his eyes fell on a painting of a young man that I now realized was a very young Saul.

"I didn't know where to go," said Saul. "I have no one else to turn to."

"I had wondered," said Mr. Landauer, almost to himself, "if we would ever *really see* each other face to face again. Seeing you at the house on that day, I had decided that all hope was gone."

"I'm sorry, Grandfather."

"No," said Mr. Landauer, "it is I who am sorry."

And then at long last it happened. They embraced each other and cried in each other's arms. I wanted to leave them to themselves but didn't want to miss the magic and happiness of the moment, so I busied myself with making coffee for Saul as they conversed.

"I looked up one day, after crying for I don't know how long, and discovered I was alone in the house. I don't even know how long ago Issa, Emma and Amber left. I can't believe I could have been so blind as to have driven them away."

"It's understandable," said Mr. Landauer.

"No, it's not at all understandable," said Saul. "I was so sure of myself for so long. And now... Now the only thing that I'm sure of is that I wrecked my life with my own hands."

"Your life is not over yet," said Mr. Landauer.

"And for that I am grateful, because I can at least say I'm sorry to you."

"No, it is I that am sorry, because whatever problems you had you learned from me."

"Discovering that everyone had left me, I didn't know what I was going to do with myself. But then I thought of you, and I knew then that you wouldn't reject me. And I thought that if I was going to try to put my life back together, this was the place to begin."

"What is your plan?" asked Mr. Landauer.

"My house is just too big for me," said Saul. "I have too many memories there. I just cannot live in that house anymore. Even to think about it is making me a little dizzy. I spent the last month alone in my head, and I just don't want to be alone right now."

"Then move in here," said Mr. Landauer. "We have plenty of room here."

"I don't want to start out by inconveniencing you of all people."

"Inconvenience? Ballard and I couldn't be happier about more company."

"Yeah, it would be great," I said, excited about the possibility of a little more entertainment around the house.

"At least until you get things worked out," said Mr. Landauer, "or until you decide that you love it here."

"Where is your luggage?" I asked.

"Well, it's in my car."

"I'll get it!" I said, happy that finally something seemed to be working out right.

Saul's moving in completely changed the dynamics of the house. Whereas before we were both a little subdued, the house now became lively and playful. We all felt, in our own way, like abandoned old men and we nourished this feeling by turning our minds towards dry scholastic pursuits. We constantly argued mundane philosophies or politics, but for us, we felt as if there could be no greater joy.

It seemed that no subjects were safe from the grips of philosophical dispute. One day when Saul sneezed, I said to him, "God bless you."

"God bless me?" Saul repeated. "In this world with so much evil, do you really believe that there could be a God?"

"Um…" I said.

"What does God care about your good and evil?" asked Mr. Landauer.

"Because," started Saul, "unless God says that it's good, or unless it's good because that's what God loves, then what other importance is there in doing what is right? But, if there is a God then how can he allow such evil to exist in this world? And if there isn't a God, then why waste our time with being good?"

"And I repeat, what does God care about *your* good and evil?" said Mr. Landauer. "These are all man-made concepts. We do good because this is a world of cause and effect and what you give you are going to get back. If you want a good life then you will treat others well."

"OOOH…Good point," said Saul.

"Well done," I agreed.

We became a house of wits. It was always a race to dissect the meaning of what we were speaking of so as to share it with our brothers. And there was no one there to tell us that we were wasting our time because we, then, only had time for each other.

Chapter 39

Issa had stopped coming to Mr. Landauer's house, and wanting badly to see her, I discovered from Mr. Cheswick that Amber, Emma and Issa had moved into an apartment near the school's side of town.

When Amber opened the door, her face immediately fell. I'd come with a heavy heart but suddenly I felt nervous for what was in store.

"Ballard?" she said, unsure of why I was there.

She opened the door to a very average looking living room with Emma and Issa seated at a table studying.

"Ballard!" Issa cried, seeing me. She jumped up and ran over. I was glad that at least *she* was happy to see me. Emma stayed at the table though, looking somber with a face to match Amber's.

"I'm so glad you came," said Issa.

"But why are the moms looking so serious?"

"We didn't expect to see you here," said Emma.

"You took him in," said Amber.

"What were we supposed to do? I thought you'd be so happy that Saul and his Grandfather finally reunited. At least something good came out of all this."

"Something good?" cried Emma. "You don't know anything, do you? You don't know what he did?"

I was a bit afraid to ask, so instead just stared, stunned.

"To Issa?" she continued.

"To Issa!" I couldn't help myself.

"Mom! Come on. It was equally my fault."

"Your fault?" yelled Emma in disbelief.

"I kept pressuring him. I wouldn't leave him alone."

"Well, he's alone now," said Amber. "Now and forever."

"He had no right," said Emma.

"What did he do?" I asked.

He hit her," said Amber with complete contempt.

What?" I stared at Issa.

"I was yelling at him and pulling on him. I just wanted him to snap out of it. I kept yelling 'Don't you care about the rest of us?' But he wouldn't move. Eventually, I was so mad that I yelled, 'You only care about that whore, and I guess you deserve each other!'"

I was shocked. I'd never heard Issa talk in such a way.

"I was going crazy too," she continued. "I just went crazy and I said what I knew would hurt him. And it did. And he slapped me so hard that I flew across the room. And then they started yelling and abusing him and he went right back into his shell. Then, Mom packed us up and we left."

"And she blames us," said Emma.

I didn't know what to think. The family that I once considered magical was now broken beyond repair.

"I'm sorry," I said. "We didn't know, but we couldn't turn him away."

"Please, just go," pushed Amber.

"It's just too hard to see you right now," said Emma.

I stared at Issa, who looked completely helpless. I could see that she didn't want me to go, but she knew that I must. She simply nodded in understanding and I left.

That night at dinner, I couldn't hold in the fact that I'd seen Issa. Still, I didn't want to accuse Saul or send him running away. So, I simply said, "I saw Issa today. I went over to their apartment."

"Oh? How are they?" asked Mr. Landauer excitedly.

At that, Saul broke down and started crying. Mr. Landauer looked at me and I softly explained it to him. Saul wouldn't have been able to hear us over the sound of his sobs. Saul buried his head on the kitchen table. Mr. Landauer squeezed his shoulder saying, "Better days must surely come." And then he got up and went to his room. After a few moments, I too left Saul to himself.

Chapter 40

If nothing else, my time in Blue Bell had taught me that reality is a matter of perspective, and for us to understand reality as a concrete truth is impossible without first changing and expanding that perspective. It takes only one moment in time to change the direction of an entire life. Destiny is the path we are set to go down, but if we simply choose to switch the road that we are on, our whole life's purpose can be instantly changed.

For me this was the night when my past met my future, and my present was illumined by an experience that was so much more real than the world of the flesh that I would not be able to live another moment without the consciousness of that experience being imprinted at the forefront of my thoughts. On this night however, I didn't feel as though I were making any choice but rather the universe was so tired of paying witness to my pathetic existence that it swooped down and started a revolution within my mind. I felt completely unprepared for what was to come. Experience is truly the foundation of any real insight into reality. Without experience, there is nothing other than ideas. But with experience comes all the possibilities that certainty provides.

My revolution, the revolution of my soul, began like any other night. I lay down for sleep in silent contemplation of the one that I felt had shattered my heart, and I just imagined what could have been. Exhausted by such thoughts, I started drifting towards that night's unconscious slumber, wanting badly just to escape into never-never land and forget for some time that I ever existed. As my eyelids grew heavy, I became aware of a buzz coming from the corner of my room. Opening my eyes, I saw that Grandma Daisy and her burning fire were right there beside my bed. I jumped up in complete alarm, but her usual stoic smile quickly calmed me down. She was sitting on the floor of my room and motioning for me to come near. I sat directly in front of her and just stared in amazement. She seemed to be singing something, although her mouth didn't move and no sound escaped her, but there was an undeniable vibration, almost a melodious hum, in the air.

For five, ten, maybe sixty minutes, I couldn't tell you, we just looked at each other. Well, I should say that I looked at her because she didn't appear to be looking at me, but rather through and around me. At least she was not looking at the me of flesh and blood, but at some unearthly part of me that she was connecting with. My head began to spin as I realized the impossibility of what I saw, and mentally pinching myself, I came to the conclusion that I was not asleep. I struggled with all my might to focus my thoughts and figure out what exactly was happening before me. Remembering that I was in my room and not out behind the school, I slowly gathered my wits about me, and finally forcing open my mouth, I asked her what it was that she wanted.

"Shhh," she whispered in a low voice. "I have not come to collect anything but to destroy the ignorance that is engulfing you. You have been given a new life, but you are clinging to the old one as if you loved it so. It breaks my heart to see you drowning in this self-created gorge of darkness and sorrow, happily drinking it in until it kills you. Seeing you march full speed down this path is too much for me to bear. You must burn this ignorance while you still have the capacity to stir the fire; or else you may enter a darkness so thick it will take you an eternity to escape."

"What darkness? What ignorance?" I tried to ask, but she put her hand to my mouth and closed her eyes as if to beg me not to talk. My mouth became cool and numb where she touched it.

Her face was very serious. Looking directly into my eyes she again began to slowly talk. Her voice was raspy and sounded as if it were coming from far away, echoing as if from the bottom of a canyon. "See this fire?" she said, motioning to her left. "This is what you need to be free. To be free of yourself. You must use it to destroy that which is chaining you to that which is not real. This is no ordinary fire though. This fire must be created in your heart. I'm talking about a fire so hot, and so bright, that no darkness can escape it. All of your illusions must be burnt up there. It is something you must do."

How to get such a fire, I thought.

"Sacrifice is the answer," she continued. "You must give up everything to gain this fire. And then you must nurture it into a bonfire that will engulf your notions of reality and light your way to heaven. Even though you don't know what you're looking for, She knows, and will arise from this fire of sacrifice."

"Who is She?" I couldn't hold back. I felt a sudden desperation to know the answer to a question that I hadn't considered until this very moment.

"That which you've been looking for but couldn't find. That which is closer to you than you are to yourself, but harder to attain than anything of this world. It is She who holds this universe together. It is She who did not let you kill yourself on that day in California. It is She who brought you to me. She is the original, the unchanging, the reason for your question. If you find Her then you will not ever have to question again. Don't waste time. She is waiting for you. She is calling for you but you are so dumb that you cannot hear Her. You must call Her and wait for Her and offer to Her what you value most, that attachment from which you are never free. You must offer Her the flower of your pitiful mind and She will give you the supreme consciousness, of which there is none higher."

I was completely dumb struck. Who was this She that until now I had never heard mentioned by anyone. I felt Daisy was telling me a great secret that I just couldn't comprehend.

"Keep quiet and listen for Her, for you can hear Her voice in the silence." This was said like a command for my life. It echoed over and over again in my head. We sat there together for sometime, and then eventually Grandma Daisy and her fire faded away, and I, bewildered and mystified, fell fast asleep sitting there on the floor.

Chapter 41

The next morning Mr. Landauer violently shook me awake.

"What is it? What is it?" I asked.

"What are you doing on the floor? You weren't moving. You didn't appear to be breathing even!"

"And you were going to shake me back to life?" I asked with great annoyance. "My head is beating like anything. Please, leave me alone."

Mr. Landauer was taken aback by my sudden burst of anger, of which I was also surprised. I immediately felt bad seeing the pain and hurt so evident on his face. I quickly recovered my senses and explained that I was just startled by this rush to consciousness.

"I just panicked is all," he explained. "You were lying on the floor covered in your own tears. What was I supposed to think? I didn't know what was going on."

I touched my hands to my face and felt the water that covered it. Upon further inspection in the bathroom mirror, I saw that my eyes were swollen from apparent hours of sobbing. I thought about what had happened last night, and not wanting to talk with Mr. Landauer about it, I hid there in the bathroom for the next hour. I sat on the floor, leaning against the tub just wondering about who this mysterious She was and how I was related to Her. And also, who was Grandma Daisy, really? At first I tried to dismiss it as a dream, but the memory of the events were so strong and clear, even clearer than those of my day-to-day life, that I was unable to reason it off in this way.

When I finally came out, Mr. Landauer was nowhere to be found, having left for his morning walk. I quickly left for my own walk in the opposite direction and just tried to recount Grandma Daisy's talk with me, word by word, trying to uncover any hidden meanings of which I could find none, nor for that matter could I even understand the non-hidden ones. I decided that the best thing to do would be to discuss it with Elizabeth. I hadn't spoken to her since she told me she didn't love me, but I felt this was more important than my pride. Still, it was early yet and the Café wouldn't be open for a few more hours. I spent the next two hours pacing a fifty yard stretch of country land thinking, and rethinking, analyzing and taking apart, putting together and adding on, and in the end was left as clueless as I started.

Eventually, I sat down completely dejected and just stared at the sky, not wanting to think about anything. Tears began to roll down my face but I couldn't explain them. I was not sad about anything in particular, but I suddenly felt as if the weight of the world was on me, and I knew that I didn't have the strength to carry it. The image of Grandma Daisy's face started to fill my mind, growing stronger and stronger until I could only see her. The pressure of her form in my head became so strong that, not knowing what to do with myself, I again passed out.

When I awoke, Elizabeth was sitting next to me with my head on her lap.

"Don't talk," she said. "Just be still for awhile. Grandma Daisy told me that she visited you last night and that I would find you here."

I wanted to tell her everything but couldn't find the strength to speak. Still, I could see in her eyes that she clearly knew what I was going through.

"Don't worry, Ballard," she said. "One day everything will be clear."

"Just tell me this, then. Who is Grandma Daisy? I mean who..." but I couldn't continue.

Chapter 42

For days I was like a crazy man. Although I did all of my duties at work, my mind was racing, trying to get a grasp on what I'd experienced. I eventually decided that I had no choice but to visit Grandma Daisy in the flesh. I was afraid to see her, though. I was scared she would say that it was all just a dream. I was scared she would say it was real. I knew only that I must find out who this She was and what duty I had to Her. So after work, I slowly walked towards Grandma Daisy's fire.

When I got close enough to see clearly, I noticed that Daisy's eyes were closed, although she didn't appear to be asleep. I didn't want to disturb her so I just sat down a few feet in front of her and waited for her to call out to me. The longer I waited, and stared at her face, the more sure I became that she was, in fact, not asleep. Her body seemed alive yet completely still, and her face was intent, though relaxed. As I waited, all of my questions arose and faded away, and I started to feel that although my eyes were open, I myself was somehow falling asleep.

The blue bells rang 1:00 a.m. and I realized that I could be sitting for quite some time. I told myself that it didn't matter how long I had to wait because I wouldn't be able to rest without getting some sort of answer from her. As I stared at her, I kept repeating in my head, "Open your eyes, open your eyes." But my effort to mentally disturb her seemed to leave her unfazed.

When the bells rang 2:00 a.m. I started to feel that Grandma Daisy was playing with me. I smiled real big for her, expecting that she would open her eyes to me at any moment, but still I was left waiting. My back began to ache and I wanted to stand up and walk around, but now I felt that this was a test and the only way to pass it was to be patient and wait till she was ready. Obviously there was nothing I could do to disturb her. There was no point, though I considered it, in making groaning or yawning noises in order to let her know that I was here and ready. She had been sitting out here for more than forty years. There was no reason why she would ever become anxious, so I remained silent and tried to show some respect in whatever way I could.

But when the bells rang 3:00 a.m. I felt that I had had enough. My mind was on overdrive as I wondered what exactly I had gotten myself into and began to mentally tell Daisy that I didn't care about her so much that I'd sit here forever. And still I sat, and sat and sat. I turned to the sky for entertainment but even the sky seemed to be asleep.

When finally the bells rang 4:00 a.m. Grandma Daisy's eyes started to open. Although they were open, I was so intent by then on Daisy's face that I didn't associate this fact with her being able to see me, or my being able to now disturb her. We stared into each other's eyes for a good five minutes before she asked me, "For what have you come? For life, or for love?"

"For truth," I said, and for the first time felt confident in my answer.

"For truth. Well that is indeed a good reason."

"Please tell me about this She. What does She have to do with me? What do I have to do with Her?"

"She is my mother and She is your mother. She's that who created you and in whom you will eventually find your home. She's the one whom after finding, you will never be in search of another. She will quench your search for truth and will be the fulfillment of your life."

Grandma Daisy looked at me for a second. Then, looking towards the sky she said, "People always ask me how I could give up the comforts of the world, and the joys of relationships. The truth is that after I found Her, there was nothing else that could compare. She's my support and my energy, my love and my life. After knowing Her all desires fell away and the pains of restlessness and hunger have been replaced by complete contentment and unending joy."

"Am I to look for Her?"

"Yes."

"Where?"

"If you want to find Her then you must attune your mind to Hers, and in doing that, She will appear to you."

"How am I to do this?"

"Elizabeth tells me that she took you to Cloverdale forest and that you heard the hum."

"Yes." I'd forgotten about this, due to the stress of more recent events, but now felt as though everything was about to become clear.

"That sound that you heard was the sound of the universe. The primordial sound. It has been there since before creation and will keep on after it is over. It can be heard anywhere in the world but in some sacred places it is louder and more accessible. Attune your mind to this sound and you will find the Mother, for the hum is Her song to us."

"But, how do I do this?" I had no idea what she meant by "tuning my mind."

"Your mind now is busy and you are unable to hear anything. You must clear your mind, let only the sound fill it, and in that silence the Mother will rise within you. Trust me and try. That is all you can do."

Closing her eyes she said, "Go to the forest and let the desire for truth fill you."

Chapter 43

I hurried home and by the time I reached there I'd decided to explain my situation to Mr. Landauer. This being the first time he was hearing about my dream, he was a bit confused and upset. He wished I would have come straight to him with such problems. Mr. Landauer knew that unusual things always happened around Grandma Daisy though, and he accepted what I said without question. He told me he would satisfy the guys at work with some excuses for my absence, until I returned, which he was hoping would be soon, although we were both unsure.

I drove to Cloverdale, parked in a place I hoped wouldn't draw attention, and slowly found my way through the thick woods to the clearing where I was to search for the Mother.

It was just about daybreak, as I looked around for a place to sit. There was plenty of room, but I felt trepidation in all directions. I didn't want to sit right out in the middle of the clearing for anyone wandering by to see. I didn't want to sit too close to the trees as I felt I would be somehow closer to all the wild animals of the forest. I eventually picked a spot next to some shrubs that were on the border of the clearing.

I sat down with folded legs and waited for a second. What exactly was I supposed to do now?

Grandma Daisy had told me to tune my mind to the sound of the hum and in that sound I would find Her. But I didn't hear the hum. To be quite honest I didn't really want to hear it yet, as I was so excited I could hardly sit still. I finally decided that I would have to burn off some of my nervous energy so I ran back and forth across the clearing for about half an hour. Finally, becoming tired, I sat back down.

I resolved then that I wouldn't get up until I found what I'd come for. Daisy had told me to sit and wait, so that was exactly what I was going to do. After another five minutes I realized I hadn't brought any blanket to sit on and was sitting directly on the grass. I then started to imagine bugs digging up through the ground and crawling on me. Where was my drive? Where was my motivation? It was slowly starting to slip away, as it dawned on me that I was a real wimp where wildlife was concerned. But thinking of my life, the life that I had left in California and the life I now had, I wondered if there was anything more important than this. It was time for me to step up and lead my mind where I wanted to go.

And so I waited. Eventually, I started to think of Elizabeth and figured that Grandma Daisy would fill her in on my situation as she had with my dream, and I knew she would be proud that I was doing something that she believed in.

Another couple of hours passed and there was not even the slightest breeze, much less a hum. Could it be that the hum was only there last time because of the presence of Elizabeth and Issa? Did it matter? My legs became numb to the point that I began to wonder if they were getting any blood at all. I again threw this thought from my mind and remembered Daisy's words that I would have to give up everything in order to attain everything. When she said I would have to give up my very life, she may have been quite literal.

Hours upon hours and still no hum. My legs felt as if they were expanding like balloons and I was waiting for them to burst open. My back was so tired that I couldn't sit up straight but had to crouch so as to rest my elbows on my legs. And what about food? I had forgotten to bring any food and all I could think of was having a nice piece of pizza.

As I tried desperately to calm my mind and listen for the hum, the day passed into night and all the forest came alive with the sound of nature. Well, what should I do now? I thought about going home for the night but figured that wasn't what Daisy meant by sitting and waiting. I was so freaked out and numb that I hardly noticed that the mosquitoes were eating me alive. Looking at my arms, I saw them sitting in a line feasting on me. I tried for a while to beat them away but eventually gave up.

Sleep was trying its best to overtake me. I was passing out every few seconds but kept jerking back to consciousness, as I would start to fall over. I kept imagining my body lying down until I started to believe that I had really fallen over. I tried slapping myself to keep my wits about me, but only during the actual slapping motion did I ever feel awake. My arms were so numb I could hardly lift them, but I felt my hands hit my face and knew that I still had some control.

Around daybreak though, the hum finally returned. Chills ran up my spine and my entire body was covered with goose bumps. I sat straight up, seemingly against my will, and I couldn't move from that position, either from fear or from some real paralysis, I didn't know. My eyes were open but my body felt shut down, unable to respond to any vain attempts of my mind to overpower it. I didn't know what I would do if I could move. So I sat there terrified by the unknown and just listened to the sound.

I tried to comfort myself with the notion that this was the sound of the Mother, but its definite unearthly nature left me feeling nauseous. Hours passed dizzying myself in this hum, to the point where I lost track of time altogether.

I was vaguely aware of the passing of days and nights, but I was under some sort of hypnotic spell. I can even remember seeing Elizabeth come and bathe me and leave some food for me, which I was unable to pick up, let alone eat. But this image of her taking care of me was like a dream. The only thing real for me was the hum.

At some point in my delirium, a little girl around eleven years old, with dark black skin, and two short pigtails, came up to me and started to rub my head. She seemed very familiar and I struggled in my haze to identify her.

"Don't worry," she said. "We are all here to watch over you."

"Who all?" I asked.

"My grandmother," said the girl. "And all of the other women of Kent."

Slowly the whole clearing filled with black women all surrounding one old woman in the center of them. They all had bowed heads while the woman in the center was speaking. But I couldn't understand what she was saying.

"That is your grandmother?" I asked.

"Yes. Don't you remember when Elizabeth told you about us?"

And suddenly I remembered how Elizabeth had said that Daisy's grandmother used to lead a group of women that would come here to worship the Mother of creation. At that time I'd been too afraid to ask of what exactly she spoke.

"Then you are Daisy?" I asked, suddenly terrified at what her answer would be.

"Of course I am."

"But how? And who are they?"

"They are all spirits of the forest now. Even you, by worshipping here, are becoming a part of this forest."

Daisy's words themselves were having a soothing effect over me, but the realization that I was surrounded by ghosts left me screaming inside. It was like a yell from deep within me that I was unable to give expression to. I was fighting to run, but my body was not responding.

And what of this little girl? Was she also a ghost? Her touch felt real, and I knew with certainty that Daisy of Blue Bell was real. But it didn't all add up.

"Where ever we go, we leave a part of ourselves behind," said Daisy. "As a little girl I used to come to this forest and a part of me has never left it behind. This is where I also first came in contact with the Mother. This is where you too will find Her."

I was no longer sure if I wanted to find Her, but it seemed as if this was out of my control. Eventually, the vision of Daisy left me and I remember struggling to gain control. I was fighting to somehow escape this insanity. But another vision, seemingly farther back in time, slowly came into focus before me.

In the center of the clearing was a giant bonfire that seemed to reach to the top of the forest. I could see thousands of ghosts or spirits circling around and around this fire and going up into the sky. The fire seemed to be alive; I felt as though I could hear it singing to me.

Slowly, one by one, I could see Native Americans, in some sort of ritual clothing, dancing maddeningly around the fire. More and more of them appeared until there were thousands of them. The sounds of loud singing and drumming were pulsating through my head, although I couldn't tell if it was coming from the people or from the fire. The dancers were completely surrounding me, even dancing over and through me. As the music became louder and louder I could see eagles circling in the sky around the top of the clearing. At first, like the dancers, it was only one or two, but then hundreds upon hundreds of eagles filled the sky. They seemed almost to be flying in rhythm to the music, in rhythm to the whole forest.

I tried to tell myself that these were spirits of the forest that were trying to help me along, but as Daisy was not there to confirm this, the thoughts became only frenzied dialogue flowing through my head, with no support and no substance. I felt myself screaming with all of my power, and a force, like that of the weight of humanity, lifting out of my body and shooting up into the sky. And then in an instant they were gone. The forest was once again calm except for the hum.

The hum now felt like my protector, my friend, my security blanket, sheltering me from all that I didn't understand. I must have sat in this calm for days, or even weeks, with only the hum filling my every thought. All that was there was the hum. No mind, no emotion, no struggle, only the hum.

And then finally, like a glorious sunrise, it happened. Arising somehow from deep within me, I saw come out and before me the most resplendent of sights. It was the Mother. There is no way to describe Her except to say that it was like looking at the sun in the shape of a mother. She was dressed in a brilliantly glowing gown, with a tall crown. Her hair flowed freely down to Her feet and Her arms were outstretched, as if calling to me. Her eyes were burning a hole into my brain so that I became completely lost in them. I became like a drunken man reveling in the splendor of Her power. I was filled with an unexplainable joy, as though I was feeling the love of the whole universe showering upon me.

And then suddenly in those eyes I saw the most horrifying of images. The Mother showed to me all of the mistakes that I had ever made, spread out over countless lifetimes, being repeated over and over again. I paid witness to every mean word, every dirty look and every harsh thought that I had ever paid out. And I saw clearly how the Mother again and again was taking different forms in my life in order to show me my faults and how I kept ignoring Her, repeating and repeating the same mistakes. The foolishness of my actions was beyond comprehension and somehow I knew that even now I would continue to make countless, thoughtless mistakes.

Eventually the images stopped and all that was left was the Mother consoling me, telling me that all was going to be all right. Completely accepting me, who after all, was Her own creation. She only wanted me to rise up to the perfected state for which I was created.

And then, she too faded away and I was left in the darkness of the forest, without even the comfort of the hum. I looked down at my body and saw that I was drenched and filthy from days of being out in the elements. I hardly recognized it as my body as I had lost so much weight that it was but a feeble replication in my old clothes. But I was too tired to think on any of this now and simply passed out.

When I finally awoke, I saw that I was lying on the ground sobbing loudly. My body was stiff, like a rock, and I was not able to sit up for about an hour of trying. Eventually though, I was able to sit and then stand, and then wobble my way back to my car. After reaching my car, I again passed into a deep sleep. Finally, awaking once more, I saw that it was night and I drove back to Blue Bell and parked outside of Mr. Landauer's house.

Chapter 44

As I sat in my car outside Mr. Landauer's house, I had to really consider how badly I wanted to make it to my own bed. I was so tired I didn't even want to consider the effort that it would take to get out of the car and walk up the pathway. I felt my whole body melting into the car seat and I had to fight to keep my eyes open. Finally, through sheer force of will, I swung the car door open. The cold night air bit my face, but even that was not much inducement. Only the thought that I couldn't let Mr. Landauer once again find me sleeping outside made me get up and start putting one foot in front of the other.

At last, reaching the front door, I leaned up against it and felt that this was good enough. I could have fallen asleep there but every time I nodded off my knees buckled, and I would start to fall down. It was only the sound of my head hitting against the door, as I nodded off, that caught Saul's attention.

I tried my best to walk casually inside, but in truth I stumbled in like a drunk man barely able to walk and unable to form any kind of greeting. Saul and Mr. Landauer had been waiting for me on a couch that they'd moved over from Saul's old place. They had tea and food waiting for me, although I had no interest in eating it, and they seemed to know already that this would be the case. We all sat down around the new living room table, another product of our new guest's move, they smiling at me and me trying to keep eye contact with them. I was physically exhausted, and emotionally unbalanced, and knowing that I could break down and cry at any moment, I wanted to quickly escape to my room.

Eventually, I gathered enough strength to ask, "How long was I away?"

"Just about three months," said Mr. Landauer.

"Three months?" I said in disbelief.

"Elizabeth came by this morning," said Saul. "She told us that Daisy said you would be coming back today."

"Three months?" I repeated.

"But don't worry. Your job is still waiting for you, just like I said it would be. You have to get the story down though." Mr. Landauer seemed extremely happy to see me, almost bouncing out of his seat. But at this moment I couldn't have cared less about my job or anything pertaining to the usual world. Flashes of scenes from the forest kept appearing in my head, making it all the harder for me to concentrate.

"Yeah, Gramps here created some real stories for you," said Saul. "He could only keep you sick for so long, you know. After a couple weeks, he changed his story, making your father suddenly ill and you having to go back to California to help him recover, even though you yourself could hardly get out of bed. Wow. How brave you were! It even made me shiver.

At any rate, those old men are pining for your return and will take you back in a second."

"Yeah, I think they're tired of cleaning your section," added Mr. Landauer.

"I'm sure you're right," I managed.

"But that Charley's a real clever one," said Mr. Landauer. "He even came over one day to visit you on your deathbed. I had to tell him that it was highly contagious and all. But he stayed and chatted about his mathematical theories, and Saul told him about his distaste for mathematics as the theories change every time you change the basic laws of space around."

"Great," I said.

"So?" Saul asked.

"Huh?" I returned

"Did you find what you were looking for?" asked Mr. Landauer

And with that the tears began to well up and I could only force myself to nod my head yes as I looked to the ground. All of the small talk seemed so useless in the wake of my vision of the Mother. I wondered how I could ever lead a normal life again.

"I suppose now is not the time to talk," said Mr. Landauer. "We are just so glad that you are back. Elizabeth brought us daily reports about you and we knew that you weren't doing well."

"I wasn't doing well?" I asked wondering what they could be referring to.

"Well," continued Mr. Landauer, "she said that you were fighting some personal demons there and that you might not make it through. That you were starving and refusing to eat, and that nature's elements were having their way with you. But that you were bound and determined not to give in."

As Mr. Landauer talked, I began to get flashes of Elizabeth visiting me everyday and bringing me food. I could see myself throwing the food back at her, and screaming and crying over all the lies that I had ever told and the ones that had ever been told to me. Still, I didn't feel like I had been acting on my own but like some force had taken over my mind and was making sure that I succeeded in my mission. I didn't know if I would ever remember fully what happened during those three months, but at this time my need for sleep outweighed the mystery.

"Well then, we'll let you get to your room," said Mr. Landauer.

"Yeah, you seem ready to pass out," added Saul.

With that I forced a smile and made my way to bed.

Chapter 45

For two days all I could do was cry. When I slept my vision of the Mother was replayed over and over in my mind. When I awoke the realization that I was suddenly alone again became unbearable. I began to hate my own skin, feeling as if it were keeping me separated from Her. I felt myself losing control over my mind. My flesh felt as if it were on fire and was burning and peeling, and I found myself rolling on the floor cursing my own existence. Was this why the Mother came to me, to make me crazy?

Then from somewhere back in the far reaches of my mind I heard a voice: "Shut it out. Save yourself. Shut it out." And this was the beginning of the end for me. Attempting to keep my sanity, I forced my mind back into the world. I thought of everything but the Mother. I started imagining what Ed and Rachel must be doing. I wondered how Saul and Mr. Landauer were dealing with my present circumstance. I thought of the other janitors waiting for my return. I thought of Issa wondering what had happened to her father. I wondered how my own father was doing, probably in jail. I began to think of Elizabeth and how she had rejected me, but realized that the thought of her only lead back to the Mother, so I even pushed Elizabeth from my mind. Then, I would start all over again with Ed and Rachel.

Slowly, over time, I became numb to the Mother, and even to my very self.

What had been the greatest experience of my life became suddenly the most terrifying. I needed to talk to Grandma Daisy, but I couldn't bring myself to do it. I couldn't take the pain that the thought of her created in me. So I decided that I would just take a few weeks to ground myself back into the world. I would take a few weeks to become normal again. Somehow, these few weeks turned into a few months, which became a few years that led into a decade of wasted time.

Chapter 46

Ten years passed without much event as my life became, through my own efforts, extremely static. I joined the college and took up philosophy and politics, but the luster that had surrounded my first year in Blue Bell slowly faded away. There were no more visions or dreams, though they were always a part of me. It is not right to say that I lived in fear of them, but more that I was ignorant as to what to do with them, and too afraid to seriously inquire any further. So, like a fool, I pushed them further and further away wanting nothing more than to become as plain, simple, and anonymous as possible.

Saul, Mr. Landauer, and myself meanwhile had become like an old man's club. We were like hermits, living only for each other and shunning the outside world. We would get up early every morning and read the paper, arguing over stories, and finding political issues in the least political of pieces. Then we would study the rest of the morning and argue all afternoon. Saul would go for a few hours a day to his office, but he admittedly didn't have to do much more than sign papers, and I would go for my same old eight-hour janitorial shift in the evening. They would both wait for me to get back home in the nights so that we could talk about what they had discovered in some books while I was away. Then we would have a cup of tea before going to our own rooms where we would sit alone and tell ourselves that we were much better off now that our lives were so simple.

With the leaving of Ed and Rachel, our connections with the others had also ended, and with that break in these friendships all of the spontaneity passed from our lives. It was not something we noticed at the time. Years passed by quickly now that I had stopped asking meaningful questions, and taken to reading meaningless answers.

Each passing day Mr. Landauer became older, while the memory of Daisy became older still. I was slowly being forced to think about the shortness of our time here. Like the others, I stopped seeing Daisy. I had made myself numb to the memory of the Mother, as the pain of not having Her constant company was too much to bear. Instead, I satisfied myself with book learning that in retrospect may have been the biggest disgrace to the gift that I'd been given. The experience I'd had in the forest was life changing, but I'd somehow missed the mark in changing my life. I knew that my life was lacking but I'd become too lazy to leave the comfort and security of Mr. Landauer's home, except to go to work.

The only other person that I kept in slight touch with was Issa, who had grown into a beautiful young woman. She no longer brought us groceries, but she still came around once a week for an early morning walk with Saul. She rarely came inside though, and most of the time I only saw her through the window. What little we knew about the others in Blue Bell came from her.

She told me of how Elizabeth had graduated from college and now had an after-school program for nearly 100 of the grade school children. Amber and Emma opened a bookstore downtown and had become a somewhat successful writing team, having had two novels published and being nationally distributed. Their subjects unsurprisingly depicted the frivolous nature of love. And it was Issa who on one morning, ten years after my vision of the Mother, brought me the most distressing news of all.

"Ballard," Issa called as she ran in from the road. "Daisy's calling for you! Daisy's calling for you!"

"What?" I asked, shocked to be hearing her name after so many years.

"There's no time to explain," she said. "We have to go now!"

"Fine," I agreed readily and we took off in Issa's car towards the school.

When we reached there, I could see clearly that someone was already with Daisy. I suspected as much, but as we got closer I could see Elizabeth holding Daisy in her arms. There were tears running down Elizabeth's cheeks and I knew this could only mean one thing. Daisy's time was over.

"My son," called out Daisy as we drew near. "Finally, you've returned. And had to be called no less." Her voice had always been feeble but now it was almost non-existent. We had to be completely silent in order to hear her.

"Still, you came right away at my request," she continued, "and that makes me very happy."

And then I too broke down and started crying like a baby. How many years had I wasted? I'd remembered the vision every day of my life but what good had it done me? I laid my head on Daisy's lap, who herself was lying on Elizabeth.

I wasn't sure if Elizabeth even knew that I was there as she was completely drawn inward into her own world with Daisy, shedding silent tears. Issa too sat completely distraught and looking beaten down as she held on to Daisy's feet.

"Sit up son," said Daisy, "I want to see you with eyes of flesh once more, before leaving this body forever."

I sat up -- helpless, unable to think. I just tried to absorb these last words and sight of Grandma Daisy, so as to store them in my memory forever.

"Son, I brought you here so as to tell you that I believe in you. That is all you need to know. Don't worry about the rest. Okay?"

I nodded my head in agreement.

Then suddenly, without warning, the hum began to fill the air. It was coming from everywhere, completely surrounding us and smothering us. No one's actions changed, but I knew all were soaking in the joy and sorrow of it. The Mother was here, and had come to take Daisy with Her.

"Elizabeth, it's time."

Hearing these last words of Grandma Daisy, Elizabeth sat Daisy back up against the tree. She looked at each of us before finally closing her eyes forever. Her body fell into ashes, and a gust of wind came and lifted this precious dust up into the air and sent it spiraling around the old oak tree, and then up and up, until we could no longer see it at all.

And with that it was done. The hum died away and a sad silence returned to us. Elizabeth and Issa became immediately absorbed in meditation. I sat with them for about an hour but eventually got up and made my way back home.

After some years, there would be few who would even believe that Grandma Daisy ever existed. But we would continue to make the old oak tree a place of daily pilgrimage and meditation, knowing that it was only through Daisy's inspiration that we had ever dared to dream of the potentiality of life, or greater still, to turn that dream into a reality.

Chapter 47

The month of Grandma Daisy's passing turned out to be a new beginning of sorts for everyone. Two weeks later, on a Saturday night, when Saul, Mr. Landauer and I were joking with each other over dinner, we heard a loud knock at the door. In those days, visitors were limited to Issa. We knew that she usually only came in the mornings so for a moment we wondered if it was more bad news. Eventually, we all made our way to the door, none of us wanting to be the first to find out what was going on behind it.

When we opened the door we were completely shocked to see two faces from our past smiling back at us with big, stupid grins. It was Ed and Rachel. Saul almost fell to the floor when he saw them, but quickly regained his composure, as Mr. Landauer and I propped him up between us. Saul had told himself for the last few years that he was long over his attachment to Rachel and his anger with Ed, but the sight of them both was too much of a shock for him to handle all at once. It didn't take too long to recover however, as the thrill of seeing these two long lost friends was equally strong.

Our laughter was as much nervous, as it was joyous, as we embraced each other. We all moved into the living room and as there was not enough room on the couch, we all sat together on the floor, except for Mr. Landauer who was too old to bend his legs like that, so sat in a chair. At first no one could talk. We just tried to soak in the image of each other, having been kept apart for so long. And then, like a flood, we all boiled over with laughter, but this time it was the sincere laughter of amazement and yearning to once again be together as friends.

"I think this is the first time you two have actually been over here," said Mr. Landauer excitedly.

"It is. It is," said Ed.

"We first went to Saul's old house," said Rachel, "but it was all locked up and looked as if no one had been there for years. So then we had a hunch that maybe if the world was indeed perfect, you would all be reunited here. And what do we find but that it is a perfect world!"

"It feels so strange to see you two," said Saul. "At first I thought I was dreaming. But now it's like you had never left."

"Indeed, it is like walking back in time ten years," said Ed.

"But you both must have gone through so much since we last saw you," I said. "Where have you been all this time?"

"Ummm... pretty much everywhere," said Rachel.

"Well, not exactly everywhere, but it's definitely a long story," added Ed.

"Please," insisted Mr. Landauer. "We couldn't ask for anything more than to hear your story. Even if it takes the next ten years for you to tell it."

"Do you have another ten years?" laughed Ed.

"Oh, you wouldn't believe the strength of this one," I said.

"Well," Rachel began. "We headed first for Chicago. It was there that we got married and that was probably the only highlight of that city."

"Hey, I liked Chicago!" said Ed. "We made a decent living working in bars there. I mean, we were young and it was fun. In retrospect, we certainly went through some hard times at first, not having much money and having to live in shady areas, but back then we didn't know it. It was our first look at what a city has to offer."

"But we could see that we weren't heading anywhere there," said Rachel. "Not that we really wanted fame or anything, but people kept encouraging us, telling us how great we were. So with their encouragement, we started to expect that we should be growing in stature and that just didn't happen. I suppose if we were left alone, we might have died in Chicago, oblivious to our condition, but it is just part of the life, the industry, the people, all keep you looking to take that next step."

"The people in Chicago said that our sound was too country," continued Ed. "They suggested we move to Nashville, saying we would definitely have a bright future there."

"Oh really?" I asked.

"Yeah," said Ed, "but it turns out our friends in Chicago didn't really know too much about the Nashville scene."

"The people there did have a lot of love for us," said Rachel.

"And I'm not saying they didn't," added Ed, "but it was basically the same story. 'You're so great. You're so great' they would say. 'But you just can't make it in Nashville.'"

"Yeah, 'your sound is far too urban to make it here,'" mimicked Rachel.

"Everyone there was telling us we needed to head for New York," said Ed shaking his head. "But come on. Us, in New York City? It was just too big for us. And there was so much competition, it was just unrealistic. Still, we fought it out there for another four years, which was twice as long as we made it in any other city."

"Anyways," said Rachel, "our friends there told us that we should try out New Orleans because our sound was so jazzy. They said we would really fit in, and that we would love the music culture of the area."

"And that was all true," said Ed.

"Absolutely true," confirmed Rachel. "We had a great time in New Orleans and the people there really loved our music. But in the end, it just came down to asking ourselves, 'What are we really looking for?'"

"Yeah," said Ed. "Everywhere we went people liked our music, but people liked our music here too. And though we had made friends wherever we went, we never had family. That is what brought us back here. We could never replace the friendships that we all shared here."

"Oh, so you came back for us?" I asked slyly.

"No, we came back for us," said Rachel. "Because of the comfort that we feel around you all. It is hard to explain, but somehow no matter how weird a family is, there is no replacing them in your life."

"Oh, I see," laughed Saul. "So you couldn't find another as weird as me, huh?"

"We could never find another like you Saul," laughed Ed.

"But in his defense," said Mr. Landauer, "Saul has changed a lot."

"Oh, I can see that," said Ed. "Just the fact that we're still here is proof enough of that!"

"Hey," said Saul, "I'm really just glad to see you all again! I'll wait until tomorrow to throw you out!"

We continued to laugh the night away and heal the scars of the past. The bond we'd once had was strong enough to overcome whatever bad feelings their leaving us behind created. And in that bond, we started to get to know each other all over again.

Chapter 48

Rachel and Ed's presence reminded us about what life used to be like, and what our lives were now lacking. They reminded us of the joy that comes from spontaneity, and the passion that accompanies living out your dreams, or at least following your heart where it takes you. We were no longer living for our dreams but rather we were dreaming about living. Over the years, we'd become so lost in the world of ideas that we abandoned the world of people. We had abandoned the thrill of being around loved ones for the security of a life without rejection and without emotion. The only joy we ever felt was in our own wits, and no longer did we experience the purer rush of emotion coming from just knowing that we were loved.

Inspired by our reunion with Ed and Rachel, we decided we wanted to reach out to all of our old friends. As we had estranged every one of them, we weren't sure if they would even come to visit the "three old hermits of Mr. Landauer's house," but we guessed that they would at least want to see Ed and Rachel. So in the name of a welcome home party, we sent out invitations through Issa, for a dinner party over at Saul's old home.

Saul's house unfortunately hadn't been lived in for ten years, and what was worse was that it had been left destroyed after Saul's meltdown. When we first walked in, we began to wonder if Mr. Landauer's house would not be a more suitable place for the party, as the magnitude of the cleanup and the history of the place were both, at first, a bit overwhelming.

"This place just brings up so many old memories," said Saul. "I don't know if Emma and Amber would even be willing to come back here."

"No," said Rachel, "they'll definitely come. You don't know how many times I dreamed about walking back into this place and seeing it again. As sick as it may seem, when we were struggling in those big cities, I would always remember all of your smiling faces. Sometimes I would want to slap your face, but still it is the memories that make this place home. Of course in none of my dreams did our house look quite like this. I guess we really did shock you all when we left."

"Um," said Ed, "maybe we don't want to bring up too many old memories."

"Don't worry Ed," I said. "We are long over it, though even I had wanted to strangle you back then."

"I know," said Ed. "And I wanted badly to tell you what was going on, but I just couldn't see making you a part of it. For one, Saul would have killed you, and for two, you might have talked me out of it; neither option seemed to be very desirable."

"Rachel," said Saul. "I can bring myself to imagine that you wanted to come back and visit, because you left on your own terms. But for Emma and Amber it wasn't quite like that. They were basically driven from here by their disgust and hatred of me. Even my own daughter didn't want to talk to me for weeks after that. Not to mention that Mr. Cheswick never looks up anymore as I pass the Café and Elizabeth always strains to smile."

"But life worked out well for them," said Ed. "We even saw Emma and Rachel's books in New York City! Those girls are big time now."

"Well, not quite big time," said Rachel. "They're still living here."

"But ten years is a long time to stay angry," added Mr. Landauer. "And I think that it was less a hatred for you and more that they were just overwrought with your pathetic state, and afraid for the effect it would have on Issa."

"And look at this house!" said Saul shaking his head. "It looks like a war zone. I can't even remember doing all of this, except for a vague picture of Amber yelling, and Emma crying and Issa running away. What kind of father, what kind of husband, was I?"

"Um... a totally self-absorbed one," said Rachel. "But that was part of your charm for awhile." We all laughed.

It took a week of hard cleaning for the five of us to get the house back into a presentable condition. We even had to hire some professionals to help rid the place of the many rodents that had taken over. But in the end, it had the same old regal look as before, minus of course, some broken paintings, mirrors and pottery that we had to cart away to the dump.

Issa even showed up to help for a couple of days, but she was mum on whether any of our friends would come. All she would say was that they were all pretty shocked to have received an invitation from us, and that they sent their love to Ed and Rachel. And I was left to wonder how I'd let my life slip into such a state that people whom I called my friends were shocked to hear from me. The level of my own complacency was puzzling even to me.

Unlike the last time, there were no cooks to prepare the food, so Rachel and I took over those duties. We kept it simple with rice, beans, lots of cheese, bread, fruit salad, and baked potatoes. We were both hoping that the love in the meal would be palpable, as the taste alone wasn't going to leave anyone wanting more. Rachel hadn't gotten any better at cooking in the ten years since she left, and though it was only for eleven people, for us it was like cooking for five hundred. We were totally over matched. But I told Rachel that burning the food only enhanced the taste, and she agreed that it also gave it a charmingly picturesque look, and home cooked feel.

When the time was finally at hand, we were still not sure whether anyone would actually show up. We all just paced around the living room expectantly with knots in our stomachs and our hands in our hair. Even Ed and Rachel had developed cause for worry.

"Did you see how Issa looked at me when she first saw me?" asked Rachel.

"I know," I said, not wanting to agree.

"She didn't know whether to smile or to cry. She was still angry with me for leaving. Of all the people, I'd thought that she would be the one to run up to me and give me a big hug. Instead, she just stood in disbelief. I must have caused her so much pain, and I'd never even realized it."

"She just didn't have time to prepare herself for your arrival," I said. "She was caught completely off guard and didn't know what to think. But she eventually became her old self and joked and played with you."

"That's true, but if even Issa had that much hesitation, then just think about what the others are going through. We were such good friends, and I just left them behind without a word, a thought or even a letter in these last ten years."

"And if they are angry with you," said Ed, "then they must really hate me. I was the one that took you away from them."

"You didn't exactly take me away."

"But that's how they're going to see it."

"Well, Ed," said Saul, "that is how I saw it, to be sure. But the girls I think will blame Rachel, not you."

"Thanks Saul," said Ed jokingly.

"Yeah, thanks Saul," said Rachel.

"They might be mad at first," started Mr. Landauer, "but I have to believe that their curiosity will get the best of them. How could they not come and see us. We mean as much to them as they do to us, right?"

"Um..." said Ed. "I hope so."

The anticipation of their arrival eventually became so great that instead of waiting for them, we decided to just keep the door open and sat down for a concert from Ed and Rachel. We decided that we might just have to make the best of things on our own and didn't want to let the clean house go to waste.

When they began to play, the music was like a divine spirit filling the house. Their music had changed so much since we had last heard them. Rachel played the piano with an aggressive passion that I didn't know she had, and her voice was now so full that it filled the whole house. When she sang, the meaning oozed from her, and we felt as if we were experiencing whatever sadness or joy she sang about. And where Ed's guitar playing had one time been rough and folksy, it now was fluent and smooth as he seamlessly interwove the many styles he'd picked up in his travels. They played off of each other like jazz virtuosos, with the aggression of rock and roll and the soul wrenching strength of gospel. We were all impressed and a little shocked that they didn't make it professionally as they'd developed all of the polish and emotion needed for their field. Still, we were happy they were back with us, and I again had visions of nice times in the park.

At the end of their third song, the room was filled with applause, but it was much more than our small group could have generated. Turning around we saw the additions of Issa, Emma, Amber, Mr. Cheswick and Elizabeth. We all immediately jumped up and what followed was a love fest of sorts. There was not one dry eye as we exchanged hugs and damned our time away from each other. Even Issa, who had until now remained stoic, cried.

Everyone talked at once as we all tried to catch up on each other's lives, all at the same time. We were so happy that we couldn't help but talk fast and endlessly. There were no hard feelings to be had, as we could no longer hold onto the pain of too many years apart. Instead, we instantly became a family again.

Eventually, we made our way to the dinner table, though the actual eating was slow as everyone continued to talk wildly. The food was merely an excuse to sit together, and luckily for Rachel and myself, nobody seemed to notice that the food was burned. This time it was Mr. Landauer who was sitting at the head of the table, with Mr. Cheswick again taking the other end. Saul, Issa, Emma, and Amber sat to Mr. Landauer's left, and Rachel, Ed, myself, and then Elizabeth sat to his right.

And after ten years of trying to forget her, I could finally talk again to the one I'd thought I'd loved. "It's so good to see you Elizabeth."

"And it's good to see you."

"There are so many questions I want to ask but just don't know where to start."

"Well," began Elizabeth, "I wanted to tell you that I was so glad you came the day of Daisy's death. It meant a lot to all of us. She'd talked a lot about you over the years, and I know she was so happy to see you."

"Happy to see me?" I asked.

"She was waiting and waiting for you for so many years, and she had said if she only saw you once more then she'd know that you would walk the right path. But she was afraid that you might never come back."

"Why didn't you call me sooner yourself?" I asked.

"I only ever called you, if she asked me," said Elizabeth looking down. "It wasn't my place to interfere. She wanted you to remember her on your own."

"Then I let her down," I said.

"No. It couldn't have been other than it was. Daisy wanted you to come because of the love she felt for you, but still she left it in the Mother's hands."

"I guess that I was just afraid," I answered, ashamed.

"That's fine," Elizabeth started slowly. "But Grandma Daisy made me promise her to give you one last message."

"Oh," I said, suddenly excited and curious, although slightly nervous. The last time Daisy told me to do something, her words had left me three months in the forest, and I wasn't as brave now as I'd been in those days.

"What did she want to say to me?"

"She told me to tell you not to waste the second chance you've been given. You've received a gift more precious than any other imaginable. You got a glimpse into the truth of the universe. You've seen the Mother in all of Her glory, but it only benefits the world if you do something with it. The Mother didn't come to you for your good fortune alone, but for the world's. You've only been serving yourself these last ten years, in all of your studies and philosophical pursuits. But only by serving humanity can you truly serve the Mother."

I didn't know what to say. I was dejected knowing I'd let Grandma Daisy down. Daisy had waited ten long years to see me, and I had only shown up on the day of her death. She'd given me the greatest gift, and I'd left her wanting.

"Don't think of the time you've lost," continued Elizabeth. "Instead, look to the time you have left to make a difference."

As she said this, the familiar blue bells rang out seven times. I couldn't help but think of how Daisy had always told me to use the bells as a motivation, remembering that I didn't know how much time I had left and not to waste it.

"Issa told me all about your after-school programs for the kids," I said.

"Has she? It's such a blessing for me to be able to give something to these kids. I'm just providing a place for them to grow, but they are the ones teaching me about life. In their innocence and their earnestness, they've shown me that truth and love is all that the mind can hope for, and all that matter has to reveal. I really don't know how I'd have gotten through these last couple of weeks since Daisy's death if I hadn't had their kindness to lift me up. I can truly see Daisy in each one of them."

"I don't suppose you could use any help there? I mean, I work pretty cheap... In fact, I can even work for free."

"I would love your help, Ballard."

"And, I would love to help you," I said. "If you see Daisy in them, then maybe I can, in some small way, repay her for all she's given me.

"Daisy doesn't want your payment, only your effort."

It was true that over all these years, I'd heard Daisy calling me. I'd dreamt of her many times. But as much as she seemed to be pleading with me not to forget, I'd been doubly intent on forgetting. I'd been unable to handle it all so fast, but I wouldn't make that mistake again.

"Ballard," started Elizabeth. "I have another question for you."

"What is it?" I asked.

"Did you ever fall in love again? Because I've been waiting for the day when I would hear of your next grand love affair!"

"Grand love affair," I laughed. "Yeah, me and myself, that was great!"

"Did you know that I see Charley all the time," continued Elizabeth, "and to this day he still makes fun of my midnight rendezvous with the great lover, Ballard Davies."

"No," I said in shock.

"How could you tell them, after you were so eager to tell me that no one had followed you?"

"Oh my God, Elizabeth. I didn't tell them anything bad about you, I promise."

"I know, I know. He told me how you came in one day asking about Ed's character! And how you hadn't recovered from my insults."

"No, I didn't take them as insults at all," I said.

"Sure, sure."

"I was just smitten in those days and over-analyzing everything."

"So you don't over-analyze anymore?" she asked.

"Well... you know."

"I know," she answered. "So. Did you ever find 'the one'?" We both couldn't help but laugh at that.

"No, never," I said. "That day you told me you didn't believe in selfish love. That was it for me. I made a solemn vow, right there in the restaurant never to give my heart again to another. I wanted to prove to myself that all of my fantasies were not merely foolish daydreams."

"Which they were."

"Yes, I know. But I still just couldn't see giving my heart to another. Not to mention that there are not too many options here."

"What do you mean?" she asked. "Emma and Amber are free." We both laughed again, to the point where the others started to look at us.

"So, I still have your heart, then?" she asked.

"Always and forever," I said.

"Hum... Same old Ballard."

"Hum... Same old Elizabeth."

CPSIA information can be obtained
at www.ICGtesting.com
Printed in the USA
FSHW010112020219
55435FS